The Future of Hooper Toote

The Future of Hooper Toote

BY FELICE HOLMAN

ILLUSTRATED BY GAHAN WILSON

CHARLES SCRIBNER'S SONS *New York*

THIS BOOK IS FOR

Herbert

JUST BECAUSE...

The Future of Hooper Toote

His mother was the first to notice it.

1

Before Hooper learned to stand, he could skim. His mother was the first to notice it. In the beginning she wasn't entirely sure, but she kept her eyes open, and one day when Hooper seemed to be just sitting on a mat playing with a rattle, she found by getting down on her knees and checking that he was actually a good half inch off the floor. It bothered her, and she put it on a list of things to tell the doctor the next time she took Hooper for a regular checkup. The list began, "Won't eat peas," and went on, "Chews his tongue," and Mrs. Toote added the third item: "Seems to skim a little above the ground."

When she told Mr. Toote about it, he chuckled in a rather annoying way and wouldn't take the time to get down on his knees and see for himself. And then, when it came time to take Hooper for the medical checkup, the doctor tapped his pencil in a please-I'm-a-busy-man tat-

3

too, and looked very skeptical when Mrs. Toote described Hooper's symptoms. But then she seemed so anxious about the skimming—even more than about the tongue-chewing—that he agreed to watch Hooper for a few minutes. But Hooper just lay quite solidly on the examination table and played with a stethoscope and smiled endearingly, while the doctor tapped his pencil some more.

"I'm afraid you just imagined it, Mrs. Toote," he said finally, speaking the line that many doctors learn their first day in medical school. And it was this attitude that caused Mrs. Toote, a reserved and pleasant woman, to come quietly to a boil, and set herself squarely on her son's side against the narrow-minded people of the earth. But she politely accepted the doctor's list of new things to feed Hooper (which included things the Tootes never touched), listened to his caution not to notice the tongue-chewing, and heard his reassurance that one day Hooper would like peas.

During the next few months Hooper grew into an entirely agreeable sort of child—hardly any trouble at all —and since he seemed quite healthy Mrs. Toote decided that there probably wasn't any harm in his skimming. As a matter of fact, it was sometimes quite convenient. For an example, it was possible, if he were skimming, to change his clothes by just slipping his shirt under him without lifting him at all from the dressing table. He scarcely mussed the covers of his crib, and he was very lightweight to carry. Even so, at first his skimming was not a steady thing—sometimes he was just plumb flat on the floor or dressing table.

But then, when he was about a year old, Mrs. Toote came into the nursery where Hooper *seemed* to be sitting on the floor quietly chewing his tongue. Beside him was a rather high pile of brightly colored cardboard blocks.

"What a lovely high pile of alphabet blocks, Hooper," said Mrs. Toote. And it was then she noticed that the pile was really much higher than Hooper could reach. And thinking it through she began to realize that Hooper was skimming a little higher than before. Not only that but now he was in contact with the floor less and less often . . . and within a very short time, *never*. She called the doctor on the phone and said she thought his condition was worsening.

"Is there a rash?" the doctor asked.

Mrs. Toote said, "You don't understand," just a bit impatiently. "He floats. He floats *off the ground!*"

The doctor was silent for a moment, though Mrs. Toote was sure she could hear his pencil tapping, and then he said, "Well, at the moment the best thing I can suggest is, when he is out of doors, tie him down."

"Tie him down!" exclaimed Mrs. Toote.

"Don't want him floating off, you know," said the doctor jovially, and laughed in a pleasant manner calculated to calm an anxious mother.

One of the many attractive things about Hooper was that, as he grew, he was completely unaffected by his ability to skim. He was neither embarrassed nor proud.

5

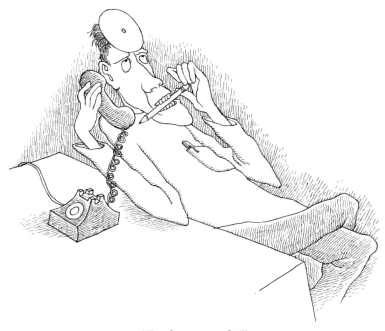

"Is there a rash?"

And as for the citizens of East Westham, a township of no great size, they were busy people with many other things to keep them occupied and interested, and they very quickly got used to having Hooper around. Mr. Toote, when he finally put his attention to the matter, simply accepted the fact that he had a son who skimmed, although he did say, "What's the good of it!"

There was one stand Mrs. Toote took quite firmly— she would not let any researchers get hold of Hooper.

Because inevitably, one day, the doctor did see for himself that Hooper skimmed. There the child was, apparently sitting on the scale, but the doctor discovered that Hooper *weighed nothing at all.* And then, of course, he was just itching to report Hooper to the medical college.

"Oh, no! No, no, no!" Mrs. Toote exclaimed. "When I first told you about it, you said that I imagined it. Now, you can just go out and find yourself another skimmer."

"My dear Mrs. Toote," said the doctor, nibbling his pencil. "Hooper belongs to research. It's your duty to let us study him and find out what it is that makes him skim."

"Hooper belongs to himself," said Mrs. Toote. "And it's not as important *why* he skims as that he be happy doing it. He is certainly not going to be happy with a whole lot of doctors prodding him and muttering about him. And furthermore," she said with unusual heat, "the next time some mother calls you and says her child is skimming, or yawing, or blipping, or whatever the case may be, perhaps you'll listen." And, one of the few times in her life, Mrs. Toote slammed a door.

Some people couldn't help guessing about it, however. Uncle Matt, who had a scientific turn of mind, guessed that Hooper might have a separate chamber in his lungs which held extra air and that this gave him just a bit of levitation.

Mr. Beedle, down the street, was an electrician and said that human beings had electrical impulses just like motors, and that obviously Hooper had a special kind of electrical reaction or a special circuit or something.

"Might be a buildup of static electricity, at the least," he said, "but more likely something like strong negative reactions in him reacting to positive reactions on the ground. Or, let's say, something to do with a magnetic field. Like that."

Mrs. Hortense Smith, who read cards and tea leaves, said it was entirely mystical, and completely explainable that way, therefore unremarkable.

Mrs. Ellie Beames, a very heavy woman, said that it was nothing more or less than the fact that Hooper just didn't eat enough.

It was years before anyone thought of asking Hooper how he did it. He thought about it carefully then and said, "Well," and pulled at a long lock of tannish hair that fell across his forehead. "If I asked you how you walk, what would you say?"

He thought about it carefully.

2

The day came to enter Hooper in the nearly new district school in the town of Central Westham. Mrs. Toote, holding his hand and enjoying, as always, the sensation of dancing with a light-footed partner, led him into the office to fill out the registration form.

"Seven," she wrote, after the question about age.

"Has already learned to read," she replied to the question of skills.

"None," she wrote in answer to the question, "Any physical reason to restrict school participation?"

But the new school clerk was walking circles about Hooper while Mrs. Toote was filling out the forms. Her eyes, Hooper thought, were marbles—lovely, glassy, absolutely perfect marbles. The fact is, the clerk's eyes were popping round only because she had come to the unavoidable conclusion that this lad applying for admission to the first grade was, so help her, *floating*. The clerk now dropped white lids over the blue marbles and squeezed them, hoping perhaps to erase an image on the delicate retina and block its path to the brain. Too late. She tiptoed into the principal's office.

"Mr. Dooey," she whispered, "I want to ask you, please, to come and look at one of the new kids. Something's wrong with him."

"How wrong?" asked Mr. Dooey, not looking up from the long list of figures that had to do with last year's fuel bills for the school heating system.

"I don't think . . ." the clerk started hesitantly. "I don't really think that he touches the floor, you know."

"Too short?" asked Mr. Dooey. "No problem. Teacher'll get him a lower chair. Several children in the same boat. One thousand and twenty-seven dollars and eighty-three cents!" He had finished adding the column of figures. "That's a twenty-three-dollar difference from the last time I added it."

"No, sir," said the clerk. "It's not that he's too short. He's . . . *off the floor, like.* Oh, please, come and see for yourself."

Mr. Dooey did not like to be diverted when he was figuring the cost of running a school efficiently. But he got up from his desk, flexed his knees, and followed the clerk into the outer office. The clerk led him across the room to the corner were Mrs. Toote was just filling in the last line of the registration form, and Hooper, neck craned, was patiently counting the squares of ceiling tile.

The clerk started her circling Indian dance around Hooper, pointing to the floor as she did it, jerking her head to direct Mr. Dooey's eyes to the focus of interest—the several inches of space visible between the bottom of Hooper's shoes and the varnished floor of the office.

Mr. Dooey's eyes still saw columns of black numerals in front of them, but even so he could not help but observe what the clerk insistently pointed out—there was a boy there who was certainly levitated. Mr. Dooey liked to think he had an open mind. Being in education, he had to keep it that way. And heaven knows, in these days, with people going to the moon and new diseases that never even existed when he was a boy . . .

"Madam," he addressed Mrs. Toote, who was just now looking up from the desk, "I wonder if you would step into my office for a moment?" Mrs. Toote smiled pleasantly and rose to follow him. Hooper started to follow, too. Mr. Dooey watched him with fascination, but then he said, "No, you wait out here, young man," and then he gave Hooper a second hard look before he led Mrs. Toote into his office.

"We shall have to consider the matter of where to place your son," said Mr. Dooey.

"He'll fit nicely into first grade for a while," said Mrs. Toote. "He is bright but a tiny bit lazy, I'm afraid."

"You don't understand," said Mr. Dooey. "I think we will have to put him in one of our . . . er . . . special classes, you know."

"How special?" asked Mrs. Toote.

"Well, the child *is* handicapped," said Mr. Dooey, deciding to come to the point.

"Handicapped! Hooper?" exclaimed Mrs. Toote.

"But surely if he can't, um . . . walk?"

"Oh, for heaven's sake!" said Mrs. Toote, relieved. "Is *that* what you mean? But why should he walk if he can *skim*?" she asked reasonably. "Why would anyone? Would you? Handicapped!" And she laughed without bitterness or derision. She was a generous person and could forgive people their narrow views.

It was a good thing that Mr. Dooey did have the open mind he had because if he hadn't, it might have taken him longer to see for himself that Hooper was in no way handicapped. For running messages (or rather, skimming messages) around the school, there was no one in a league with Hooper. Where other heavy-footed boys stomped through the halls with notices of early dismissal, health inspections, fire drills, et cetera, from teacher to teacher, Hooper glided quietly from class to class distracting no one from his work.

His own teacher prized him for erasing blackboards. He reached higher, did a neater, smoother job than anyone. As for Hooper, he was delighted to be excused, from time to time, from the more concentrated work of adding and subtracting. And he was very happy and outgoing. Always a gregarious boy, friendly, generous, and generally well-liked (except by the jealous), he was

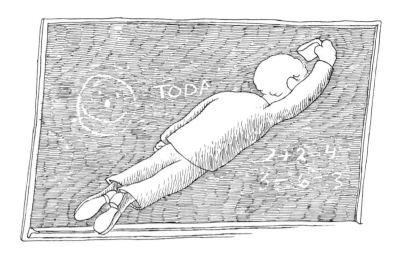

His own teacher prized him for erasing blackboards.

now surrounded by more people than he had ever known. Even the girls were nice to him. And he was popular when they jumped rope. He could beat anyone at jump rope.

As time went on, the practical aspects of skimming were apparent to anyone who would take a moment to think about it. Crossing mud puddles was just one, and Mrs. Toote appreciated it, especially since Hooper never made any muddy footprints on clean floors.

It was not until Hooper was ten that a very surprising thing happened. Hooper had his first attack. And for want of a better term, they were always called attacks after that. It was during a spelling bee. Hooper was one of the two boys left. The other boy was Morty Shwester. The word was "friable." Hooper started to think very hard. "F-R–" he began. He chewed his tongue and stared at a cobweb on the ceiling while the teacher's forefinger stiffly held the place on the page. Hooper thought, now was it Y, which is how you spell fry, of course, or was it . . . ? And Hooper continued to stare at the cobweb on the ceiling. Was it a cobweb or just some dust? It was hard to tell at this distance. He didn't see any spider. It was wispy, like a tiny cloud. A tiny cloud on the ceiling of the classroom. As Hooper stared at it, it seemed to get larger. He could see quite clearly now that it was a cobweb. Quite a big one and not as pretty as it looked at first. And at that moment his head hit the ceiling.

"Hey!" he said, and looked down.

All eyes were turned upward, all mouths agape, as they had been the whole time Hooper had been slowly skimming higher. As soon as she was able to speak, the teacher decided to take a firm tack.

"Hooper Toote," she said sternly. "You get down here right now."

"Yes ma'am," said Hooper, but try as he would he could not manage to think of a way to come down. He tried breathing in and he tried breathing out, but up he stayed.

"You heard me, Hooper," said his teacher. "This is a very shabby attention-getting device. If you can't spell a word, admit it. You don't have to carry on like that."

"No, ma'am," mumbled Hooper, a trifle embarrassed

now. And he reached out absently and flicked the cobweb off the ceiling. It drifted softly down and fell onto
the teacher's forefinger, which was still pointing firmly
to the word "friable." Following the web's fall from his
height, Hooper, squinting, thought that the next letter
seemed to be an I. It didn't seem to branch out like a Y.
Or did it? He felt like a cheat . . . horribly guilty, but
before he could make up his mind, the teacher shook off
the cobweb with annoyance and said, "Friable, Morty?"

"F-R-I-A-B-L E, friable," said Morty Shwester, without any hesitation whatever. However, the cheers he
would have received for his triumphant win were not so
great as they might have been. Hooper was upstaging
him.

"Very well. Come down now, Hooper," said the teacher.

"I can't," Hooper said. "The fact is, I don't know how
I got up here and I don't know how to come down. It's
the first time it's happened."

"Truly?" exclaimed the teacher, beginning to see she
had been wrong in suspecting Hooper of merely bidding
for her attention.

The class really came alive at this point. "Hey, Hooper!" cried Curly Green, "You're sure lucky this room
has a ceiling!"

"Not as lucky as the kids in the class above us," said
Morty Shwester, the brain. "If we didn't have a ceiling,
they wouldn't have a floor!"

Hooper smiled down pleasantly, though a bit confused
and embarrassed. And then the cheering, laughing, and

15

delighted children were brought to the end of their school day by the bell.

"Dismissed!" cried the teacher, keeping her eyes on Hooper. "You stay right there," she said to him. "I'll go and tell Mr. Dooey."

And she did. And Mr. Dooey called Mrs. Toote, and Mrs. Toote hurried over.

"I'm sorry," Hooper apologized to his mother. "I don't know how it happened."

"What were you doing at the time?" asked Mrs. Toote, keeping her wits about her.

"Nothing, really," said Hooper. "I was just down there trying to think of how to spell 'friable' . . ."

"Friable!" exclaimed Mrs. Toote. "What kind of word is that for a ten-year-old boy!" She looked at the teacher questioningly.

". . . and I was thinking about it and not noticing anything until I hit my head," Hooper finished.

"Your head! Oh, Hooper, are you hurt?" Mrs. Toote's mother instinct was strong.

"Not a bit," said Hooper.

Mrs. Toote, relieved, turned her attention to the teacher. "How is Hooper doing?" she asked.

"Well, he's a bright boy," the teacher said, "but not overindustrious, let us say."

There was a laugh from the ceiling. "You all look pretty funny from here," Hooper said, seeming quite relaxed.

"It's not a laughing matter, Hooper," Mrs. Toote said.

"Now, now," said Mr. Dooey, in a quiet aside to Mrs. Toote. "Let's not seem to be showing him too much attention."

"Attention!" said Mrs. Toote. "But how is he to come home for supper?"

"Well, this problem is really not so difficult," said Mr. Dooey, taking over as an administrator should. "I'll get a ladder and take him down."

The next attack really raised a ruckus. Popular or not, Hooper did get into an occasional tangle with one or two of the boys in his class, just now and then. Usually it was nothing much—the kind of thing he could handle as well as the next fellow. But one day, out on the playground at recess, he got into a fight that started out like nothing and ended up like something. His opponent was one of the bigger boys, and as the hassle started, they exchanged a few tentative taps. Hooper returned tap for tap, until it started to warm up. It warmed up rather suddenly, with the big boy landing a hard punch on Hooper's arm. Hooper missed entirely with his next punch, landing it somewhere in the air around the boy's neck. The big boy was doing some fancy footwork now, starting to enjoy his superior position. Then Hooper started wishing he was one of those really great fighters in a real ring. He could beat the devil out of this boy if he had even half the muscle of a guy like Jack Dempsey or one of those old-timers. This boy would be lying flat on the canvas and someone would be holding Hooper's own hand in the air, yelling "The winnah!"

And then, just when the bigger boy was about to land a strong left-hand punch, Hooper seemed to slip up out

Hooper seemed to slip up.

of position, as if greased. And then, rather rapidly, he skimmed well up above the reach of the fighting tiger below . . . and just stayed there.

A good many feelings about Hooper went tearing around the playground—astonishment and anger on the part of the stormy opponent; but by and large, most children felt either admiration or envy, depending on their personalities. It was a truly unusual recess.

As for Hooper, himself, this was his first experience in outer space, so to speak, and his feelings were mixed. He was surprised, relieved, somewhat exhilarated, and slightly embarrassed; embarrassed, because there seemed to be no way to get down. Mr. Dooey came out to shoo the children back to their classes, and Mr. Toote was called. There was no place to lean a ladder this time, so Mr. Dooey and Mr. Toote just stood in the playground talking things over. The children stood at the classroom windows and not much work got done.

But it soon became apparent that time would take care of the problem. Little by little, ever so slowly, and over a period of a couple of hours, Hooper lost altitude, and by the time school was out, Hooper was down to his normal skimming height.

"Don't do that again!" said Mr. Dooey, forgetting about the fight.

"No sir," said Hooper, grabbing his father's hand. But the fact was, he wasn't sure about it.

3

Shortly after that, when Hooper was just past eleven, Mr. Toote was transferred to his company's office in New York City. They selected a nice apartment on the third floor of an attractive red brick building facing a tree-lined street, and Mrs. Toote, though very sorry to leave all her kind friends in East Westham, was pleased with the prospect of the exciting new life of the city. Hooper, too, was touched with great regret and pleasure which equalized each other nicely and put him in a perfect frame of mind for the big move.

The first few days of the early summer were spent just getting used to things and places. On Sunday, Mr. and Mrs. Toote and Hooper walked (or skimmed, as the case might be) up and down Fifth Avenue, up and down Madison Avenue, across some of the streets from river to river, down around Times Square, up Broadway, and then into Central Park, just getting their bearings. But they soon discovered that an unexpected and rather disquieting thing seemed to be happening. Whereas the people of East Westham had accepted, without undue astonishment or comment, the skimming of young Hooper Toote, the people of New York did not seem to be able to ignore it.

"Really!" said Mrs. Toote, "I thought New Yorkers were supposed to be so sophisticated! You'd think Hooper were bright blue or something! Really!"

"I don't know," Mr. Toote said. "They tell you New Yorkers walk along without seeing a soul around them, but every one of them seems to gawk at our Hooper. It's sure annoying, I'll admit it."

They talked about it all the way back home, and then when they approached their apartment building, Mr. Toote reached into his pocket for his keys. Not there! "Blast!" he said. "Left the keys in my other suit. You've got yours?" he asked his wife.

Mrs. Toote looked concerned. "No," she said. "I'm sorry. I thought you would have yours, you know."

"Well I suppose we can get a duplicate from the superintendent," said Mr. Toote. So they went to the rear of the apartment lobby and saw a note on the super's door. "Back at five o'clock."

"Five!" cried Mrs. Toote. "That's three hours away. Oh dear!" They went out and looked up at their windows, not twenty-five feet away, shining brightly in the Sunday sun.

"There must be some way," said Mr. Toote.

"Perhaps you could let yourself down on a rope from the roof," suggested Hooper.

"Ha!" was Mr. Toote's reply. "You'll have to think of something better than that." So Hooper started to think of something better, staring up at the windows. He thought of going down into the cellar to see if there might be a ladder, but it would have to be an awfully long ladder. And that made him think of the fire department and that they might come and use their long ladders. Oh, those were marvelous long ladders. He'd seen them on his tours of the city. Wow! He would really love to go up on one of those ladders, wearing one of those shiny raincoats and those great hats and boots, and maybe save someone who was . . .

Mr. Toote emerged from his own deep thought and looked up. He found he was looking at the soles of Hooper's feet. "Mercy!" he said.

"Oh, Hooper! Another attack!" cried Mrs. Toote. "Grab him, Hugh!" But Hooper was out of reach.

Hooper looked down in surprise. "Hey!" is all he said.

"But, Hooper," said Mrs. Toote, "you can't just stay there."

"No," agreed Hooper, "but it may be a long time before I drift down."

"Oh dear," said Mrs. Toote. "How boring for him, Hugh. Maybe you could tell him a story to amuse him."

"Okay," said Mr. Toote, "but it's so far to yell. Maybe I could just give him a good riddle to keep him occupied."

22

"Okay," called Hooper, making the best of the situation. "Shoot!"

"Now let's see," Mr. Toote thought aloud. "Ah, here's one that I remember. A sultan had fourteen wives and three thousand eight hundred and ninety-six pieces of gold. If each wife had four children, how many pieces of gold would each child have, if the money was divided equally among them?"

"What country was that?" asked Hooper with interest.

"Hugh!" reproached Mrs. Toote. "Fourteen wives!"

Hooper was working on the problem. It was hard to do in his head. He used his hand to write the numbers in the air. First, fourteen by four. That was . . . um . . . fifty-six children. He checked it. Okay, now what do you do? You've got these fifty-six children. Fifty-six children! Hooper, an only child, thought delightedly of the fun of fifty-six brothers and sisters. Imagine the dinner table with fifty-six children around it, all wanting the drumsticks of the chicken! Imagine the games! Imagine all the Christmas presents and birthday parties. Why, there would be at least one birthday every week, probably! He turned to ask his father how many girls and how many boys. He was in for a surprise. The street was much farther away.

At the same instant, Mr. Toote was shouting "Hooper! Hooper, you've skimmed right up to the window. Grab hold of the sill!"

"Why, that's our apartment!" cried Mrs. Toote.

Hooper acted quickly. He reached out and grabbed the

sill of their own living-room window. Then he pulled himself over and rested against it. Then he turned and put his weight against the window sash and pushed at the window. It didn't budge, but Hooper did. His foot slipped, and he was off in space.

"Hooper!" screamed Mrs. Toote. But Hooper was safe as a baby in bed. He stayed right on a level with the window, maneuvered back to the sill, and heaved again. The window opened bit by bit. Hooper was just about to slide over into the living room when a voice from the ground yelled, "Hold it!" and Hooper nearly lost his footing again as he twisted around to see what was what.

What-was-what was a young man on the ground aiming a 35-mm camera with a telescopic lens at Hooper. "Smile and wave," he yelled.

Hooper, who usually smiled, though seldom had occasion to wave, disliked on principle to do it on order, and so he frowned. He turned his back on the whole situation and slid over the sill into the nice cool living room.

On the ground, however, Mr. and Mrs. Toote were now besieged by Sunday walkers.

"How did he do it?"

"Is he on a rope?"

"Has he got a motor or something?"

"Is that a space suit he's wearing?"

Mrs. Toote was thoroughly disgusted. "You should all be ashamed of yourselves," she said. "Carrying on like that! Is life in the city so humdrum and dreary that any little thing out of the ordinary causes a sensation? Haven't

24

the people of New York ever seen a . . . a sunset?"
She nudged the young man with the camera. "Well,
have you?"

"Yes, sure," he said.

"Well, if you've seen a sunset, you've seen one of life's
dramas. Why should anything else cause you that much
consternation? Come on, Hugh," she said, and shrugging off the people, she went inside the apartment building.

Hooper had unlatched the apartment door for them,
and Mrs. Toote, still uncharacteristically annoyed, led
the way into the kitchen and poured iced tea for everyone.

Hooper went over to the window and stared out, taking long, cool, tan sips of tea. The crowd was still there
and new arrivals were collared and informed of the interesting happening by the first-comers. There was
much pointing and gesturing, and loud voices rose to the
third floor. "There he is!" shouted one, catching sight
of Hooper in the window. Hooper faded back into the
room.

Mrs. Toote began to cry, and for a controlled and
sensible woman this was a true measure of her trial.
Hooper went over and patted her shoulder, "Don't cry,
Mum. It's not so bad. It might even be . . . interesting."

Mrs. Toote looked up. "My brave little son," she said.
Then, "Oh Hugh," she sobbed to her husband, "this is
what I was afraid of when the doctor first wanted to have

researchers look at Hooper. I want him to have just a normal, happy life."

"Don't worry, Mum," said Hooper, in whose mind a new vista of life was just beginning to shape up. "I think I can handle it."

"Listen," said Mr. Toote, as he looked down at the excited crowd. "Why ever it is that Hooper skims, I think we had better think about . . . um . . . well, hiding it, or disguising it for a while anyhow. It seems to upset people a lot around here. What we need is a controllable situation to keep him from skimming up so far and attracting that much attention."

"Oh dear!" cried Mrs. Toote at even the *thought* of having to go through the recent ordeal again. "What can you do, Hugh?"

"Nothing to fear," said Mr. Toote. "For the time being, I'm just going to get him some calibrated weights to hold him down. I'll do it as soon as the shops open in the morning. It's as simple as that."

Then the phone started ringing, and it didn't stop for hours. First it was the people from *Mannish Magazine*. Pictures were what they wanted. Sums of money were mentioned. Mrs. Toote said, "Hooper is boyish, not mannish." And then she said, "Two thousand dollars!"

Hooper started figuring how many marbles that would buy, and although he was still skimming considerably higher than usual, Mr. Toote thought he was losing altitude. All the same, he said, "Let's just get that flatiron

26

for you to hold, Hooper, to sort of try out my idea."

He went in and got the iron and a big, old griddle, too, and gave them to Hooper. "Okay!" said Mr. Toote, seeing that Hooper had returned to his normal skimming height. "It works."

The next call was from the *New York Daily*. They wanted an interview. An exclusive. Hooper, a polite child who did not ordinarily interrupt, talked into his mother's ear while she was on the phone. "Tell them we'll think about it," he urged.

"Hooper!" cried Mrs. Toote.

"Is that his name?" asked the reporter on the phone.

"No comment," said Mrs. Toote, and hung up.

They drew the heavy drapes at the windows and sat in the shadowed room sipping iced tea and being rather glum, for the Tootes. Mrs. Toote was the most depressed of all. Hooper sat in a large upholstered chair, clutching the flatiron and griddle, contemplating a number of stimulating thoughts, such as adding up the offers made by the newspapers and magazines, and thinking what he would do with the money. And that reminded him of the problem his father had given him about the sultan and his numerous wives, but some of the details escaped him. Something about all this excitement seemed to aggravate his condition to the extent that his father found it necessary to put a rather heavy set of history books on top of the flatiron and griddle.

"It's nerves," said Mrs. Toote, very concerned.

After that climactic day, Mr. Toote, who had kept generally out of it during the early upbringing of his son, now came forward with a number of practical suggestions. They were appreciated by all.

"In the first place," he said, "while we know that Hooper's skimming is not a disadvantage, and is often a plus, it is not really pleasant to be causing heads to turn. Is it? Therefore I think the best thing, here in New York, would be to try and melt into the crowd whenever possible, for a while anyway . . . just for the expediency of it." He took a breath.

"Animals have protective coloration," he went on, "and Hooper could use this same principle. Now, for walking on the street . . ." And that is when Mrs. Toote, at her husband's suggestion, designed the extendable trouser leg. It was a sort of extra-sized cuff which let down over Hooper's feet and touched the ground when he was just at his normal cruising height. And, while it did make him look like a very long-legged boy with extraordinarily small, indeed invisible, feet, it was less distracting than a boy skimming down Fifth Avenue. Mrs. Toote, also at her husband's suggestion, made the jacket a bit longer so that it covered the space between Hooper and the chair when he was seated. These tailoring alterations, plus the calibrated weights that Mr. Toote devised to slip into the jacket pockets, certainly seemed an immediate solution to Hooper's main problem.

While Hooper's skimming wardrobe was in preparation, there was an air of what might be called intrigue about the house. People still gathered below the window, craning their necks. The phone rang frequently, and went unanswered. Mr. Toote used the fire stairs to slip out of the house to his job, and then did the family marketing on his way home. He pulled his suit collar up around his face as he slipped back into the building, and he also acquired an old pair of aviator's goggles in a thrift shop, which tended to throw people off the scent.

Nevertheless, there were a few unpleasant incidents to mar the quiet retreat. In one case it was the return of Mr. Toote from a shopping expedition, carrying a newspaper which featured a very disturbing article. HUMAN FLY? was its headline. The story stated that an amateur photographer had presented the newspaper with a photograph of something that the photographer claimed to be the "human fly" which, he insisted, upheld the contention and testimony of many people on the street that there had been a feat of levitation performed on the east side of the city. In the absence of real evidence, the newspaper had to suspect that the picture was faked, and feared that this kind of rumor was the sort of thing to bring in whole batches of such false photos, only causing more crowds to collect and more rumors to start.

Hooper gave a great loud laugh, and then another. "Human fly!" he choked between laughs. "Human fly!" And he skimmed about a bit, flapping his arms, and made a few useless attempts to climb the wall.

But Mrs. Toote was irate. "That poor fellow," she

said. "That was a perfectly honest photograph. I'm sorry I scolded him, now. I have a good mind to call that newspaper and tell them a thing or two. My, that poor man must feel bad!" But she thought better of it when Mr. Toote pointed out that calling the newspaper would only draw more attention to Hooper and this was what they were trying to avoid.

"Oh dear, I guess you're right," said Mrs. Toote. "But it's still not fair, and I don't feel right about it."

The next unpleasant thing changed Mrs. Toote's feelings of regret entirely. Garbed in working clothes, the photographer let himself down the side of the building on a window washer's rig and shoved a camera through the drapes of the open window of the Tootes' apartment. Mrs. Toote screamed, Hooper ducked, and Mr. Toote approached the window with the business end of a floor mop. The photographer disappeared in one twenty-fifth of a second, pulling his rig up to the roof as fast as a rig could be pulled. That was the last they heard of him . . . for a while.

Hooper spent his time of seclusion within the apartment skimming about aimlessly, peeking from behind the heavy drapes, and feeling generally restless and quite frustrated. Mrs. Toote thought she would keep him busy and, at the same time, get a few needed chores done while she was occupied with the suit. The first morning she said, "Hooper, I wonder if you could dry those

He shoved a camera through the drapes.

breakfast dishes for me, please, while I get on with the trouser cuffs?"

Hooper, though an agreeable boy, was not really any keener on dish-drying than most boys, but he said,

"Okay," and took up a dish from the drainboard. As he started to dry it, he skimmed over to the window and looked out at the little iron balcony on which Mrs. Toote had started a small window box of herbs and mint. Three floors below was the apartment courtyard that Hooper had not yet investigated. It occurred to Hooper that one of the advantages of the city was the many expanses of pavement for bouncing balls, for example, for playing four-square and hopscotch—things you could only play on the school playground at East Westham. He leaned out of the window to take a look. A whiff of mint from the window box tempted him. He reached for a leaf. It was just a bit too far out. He reached a bit further and was in a somewhat seesawish position—half in and half out—when Mrs. Toote's small scream from the kitchen door sent the dish sailing out of Hooper's hand and crashing into the courtyard.

Hooper skimmed back in. "I'm sorry, Mum," he said. "And that dish was really dry. I mean, I really dried that dish."

"Never mind," said Mrs. Toote. "But you're not to go out. You do understand that, Hooper? And stay away from the open windows, please!"

"I wasn't thinking," said Hooper.

He wandered around restlessly once more until Mrs. Toote suggested that he might like to run the vacuum cleaner for her. The suit was taking all the time she would normally spend tidying her house. "Just for looks, Hooper. Don't try moving the furniture or anything."

So Hooper switched on the floor vacuum and buzzed back and forth, back and forth. He got a certain kind of satisfaction as he whipped up the clippings from the sewing and gobbled them into the belly of the vacuum. "I'm a great hungry dragon," he told himself. But then the flower pattern of the rug suggested another notion, and as the vacuum buzzed from flower to flower, Hooper fancied himself a very modern, highly mechanized bee. He whipped around faster and faster, zooming from roses to peonies, gaining speed. And then there was another cry from Mrs. Toote, who had looked up to find Hooper lying straight out in mid-air behind the vacuum, knocking over a lamp as he flew past. She hurried over and pulled the vacuum cord out of the socket, and Hooper came to a sudden stop in the middle of a rose.

Mrs. Toote could see that Hooper's usefulness as a household aid was limited. It wasn't that he wasn't willing, she had to admit. It just seemed easier, on the whole, to do things herself, when she got the chance. Less wear and tear, she thought, licking a piece of thread and aiming at the needle.

And so then Hooper would go and sit in the deep chair and try and think about something that seemed to be naggling in the back of his brain. Whenever an attack seemed to be coming on, Mrs. Toote would hurry over with the griddle and pile on the flatiron and the big volumes of H. G. Wells, which were always handy for that particular purpose.

Well, it is strange how things happen, but it now

seems probable that it was this waiting period that was the turning point in Hooper's life. One day the history book fell open to a chapter about the Normans, the Saracens, the Hungarians, and the Seljuk Turks, and quite out of boredom Hooper started to read it . . . and for the next three days he read avidly and constantly.

Quite oddly, whenever he put the book aside he felt hungry, and Mrs. Toote would put down her sewing and bring him all kinds of appetizing morsels—eggnogs and chicken soup.

Much later in life, when Hooper had become a thoughtful man, he sometimes ruminated on the chain of events that had brought him to that point in his life—how one thing balanced on another, how one thing triggered the next—and he felt able to say that the strongest catalyst to his life was the fact that his father had forgotten his key, and *that* had unquestionably led to the other significant changes in his life patterns. Hooper tried never to allow himself to think how his life might have turned out if his father had not forgotten his key, or if his mother had remembered hers, or if the superintendent had been home, or if no one had been passing by at the time, or if Mr. Toote had brought *not* the history by H. G. Wells but had brought instead, let us say, the New York telephone directory.

Sometimes, sitting in the chair, resting his eyes from all the unaccustomed reading, Hooper started to do a bit of creative thinking. The naggling in the back of his brain broke through to the main thinking area. Hooper, always having been of a rather relaxed and well-adjusted nature, had up to now been quite content with the status quo. The present had always been enough—pleasant, warm, and affectionate. But during the last few days in New York, something new had come into his life. Part of it was, he decided, his advancing age, now coming up onto twelve. But part of it was something strange, something electric, something exciting that beckoned and gestured, that shouted to him, and *this*, he decided (though not in so many words) *was the future.*

4

When the new suit was completed and Mrs. Toote had bitten off the last thread, it was really well worth the tiresome wait and the days of confinement. It was enormously practical. It did the job admirably, and quite beyond that, it was a sartorial delight.

The day the suit was finished, Mrs. Toote threw back the heavy drapes, opened the windows and let the sun and air come in. Mrs. Toote smiled at Mr. Toote for the first time in several days, and they stood at the window, taking deep breaths of the seemingly fresh air that blew from Central Park, over the treetops, down the side streets and into their apartment.

Hooper, himself, was raring to go! He tried a few experimental skims about the apartment, just testing, and was immensely satisfied. Mr. and Mrs. Toote, turning from the window, looked at him proudly, and Mrs. Toote said, "Hooper you look so tall! And really very . . . very nice!" Hooper ducked his head in appreciation and then scooted out of the apartment. He had just rung for the elevator when the Toote door was flung open and Mr. Toote came rushing out holding a package.

"Glad I caught you, son," he said. "Here's a little present." He laughed almost shyly, and pushed a medium-sized box at Hooper. It was surprisingly heavy.

Hooper loved presents and this was a really gala and exciting day, anyway. He tore the wrappings from the box and then, placing it on the floor, removed the cover.

"Roller skates!" he exclaimed.

Mrs. Toote had joined them in the hall. "Roller skates!" she echoed. "Oh, Hugh, why on earth does Hooper need roller skates? It's the last thing he needs."

But Hooper was looking at them speculatively. In the small town where the Tootes had lived, roller skating was not a popular sport for the simple reason that the sidewalks were few and far between and seldom continuous.

"You try 'em," said Mr. Toote, bending to help Hooper adjust the skates to his shoes. "It was just a little idea I had. A sort of double-purpose idea, you see. See how it works." He helped Hooper to his feet.

The significance of Mr. Toote's idea was immediately evident. The big ball-bearing wheels of the roller skates filled the space between Hooper's shoes and the floor perfectly. For the first time, Hooper was standing right on the ground—or at least, his skates were.

Mr. Toote was excited. "Not only that," he said, "they're heavy, see. They act as a bit more weight when you need it."

Mrs. Toote smiled. "Hugh, that was very thoughtful. Very."

And then the elevator arrived and Hooper, rolling unsteadily, entered. He clutched the handrail for support, pushed the lobby button, waved to Mr. and Mrs. Toote, and then the doors shut.

When the doors reopened, Hooper shuffled out of the elevator into the lobby, grabbing at chairs and tables to steady himself. The new experiences coming so fast were a bit unnerving. The feel of the ground beneath his feet was quite enough, but the experience of stumbling, when gliding was more his style, was quite shocking.

Through the open front door he could see people hurrying by. Hooper's stomach was clutched by something like nervousness, but then his eagerness to get going pushed the feeling away. He straightened his back (nearly losing his balance while doing so), thrust his chin forward, and assuming an air of what he thought might project cool collected casualness, began to skate rather unsteadily out the lobby door, onto the sunny street.

Hooper skated, after a fashion, straight through the scattering of people and along the street that led to the park. Crossing Madison Avenue was somewhat nerve-racking for Hooper, himself, as well as for observers who had every reason to believe he would never make it. But he did, and by the time he had reached Fifth Avenue he had acquired some, if not all, the skills necessary for safely indulging in the sport of roller-skating.

The sight of the park's greenery, after his indoor con-

The new experiences coming so fast were a bit unnerving.

finement, refreshed and stimulated Hooper enormously, and he accelerated his skating and was able to swoop down a slight incline and into the winding sylvan paths of the park with a minimum of arm thrashing. It astounded him to find how much harder it was to maintain balance on the ground than in the air, and he gained a new respect for the rest of humanity which had to master that skill. It crossed his mind—just a passing thought—that actually he was the only skimmer he had ever seen! Was he the only one?

But Hooper was not the only skater. The sloping walks attracted other young sportsmen and sportswomen, and Hooper sat himself on a bench to do a bit of observing. There were some tricks to executing the turns, he could see that. It could be simple or showy and quite beautiful. Skating on one foot was also a higher form of the sport developed by some of the more extroverted youngsters, and it did get quite a lot of attention for them from the girls. It looked like a lot of fun. A few of the children gave him shy smiles as they skated by, and before long Hooper rose unsteadily to his feet and joined them. He wasn't at all bad. Nothing admirable, but not bad for a beginner. A stocky boy yelled, "Hey, catch!" and tossed a small ball at him as he swooped by. Hooper missed it, but then retrieved it and pitched it back with a laugh. The boy skated over and squinted at Hooper through rather thick glasses. "Never saw you around," he said. "You from around here?"

"I'm from East Westham," said Hooper, "but we've

just moved to New York. I'm Hooper. Hooper Toote."

"My name is Blue," the boy said. "My real name is Herman Bluestone, but they call me Blue. I can't help it," he shrugged. "Anyhow, it's better than Herman. And *anyhow*," he became suddenly a bit sullen, "Hooper is a pretty funny name anyhow."

"Is it?" said Hooper. "I suppose it is. *Hooper*," he said to himself. "Maybe it is. I'm used to it. Anyhow, I didn't say Blue was a funny name."

"You were probably thinking it. Right?" asked Blue.

"I don't know," Hooper answered truthfully. "It doesn't seem all that funny. I know a fellow back in East Westham whose name is Red. That's not so different from Blue. I know a guy whose name is Sidney."

"What's the matter with Sidney?" asked Blue.

"Nothing," said Hooper. "That's what I mean."

Blue gave Hooper a friendly punch on the shoulder. "See you around," he said.

"See you," said Hooper, and he started skating uphill —a bit of a trick, but he managed to do it marvelously. He followed his long shadow, which was moving oddly ahead of him. Life in the city, he thought as he skated, might really turn out to be very well suited to a person who happened to be a skimmer.

41

5

There were many things about Blue that made him an interesting companion. For one thing, he was city-born and city-bred and he knew the streets of New York like Hooper knew the streets of East Westham. The mysteries of the city became less mysterious under the able guidance of Blue.

One early morning, as they skated along, a girl called, "Hi," and Blue muttered something that might have been "Hello," and then, since the girl and her friend were standing right in the path, Blue stopped and introduced Hooper. Blue looked straight at the ground and waved his arm in the general direction of the girl who had said "Hi"—a very tall and graceful creature with reddish-brown hair and, Hooper thought, eyes to match. She had noticeably long eyelashes.

"This is Athena," Blue said, and he sort of whispered it, or else his voice had a frog in it.

In response, Hooper whispered, "Hi."

Athena waved her lashes and said, "This is October,"

and she pushed her friend forward. October smiled at Hooper and Blue.

Then Athena said, "I think one day soon I am going to sail a boat on the sailing pond," and she seemed to say it to the air, "only I don't have a sailboat."

And Blue said, "Oh." And then they all stared at each other for a while and shuffled a bit. And then Blue started backing off, skating, and Hooper said, "Bye," and skated off, too.

As they skated away, Blue was sort of rosy. "What d'ya think?" he said finally.

"Think about what?" Hooper asked.

"Her," said Blue a bit impatiently. And then he started whispering again. "Athena. What d'ya think of her?"

"Hey, does she have red eyes?" asked Hooper.

Blue looked like thunder and lightning. "Red eyes!" he shouted. "Are you out of your mind? She has *golden* eyes! Golden eyes, and golden lashes."

"Oh," said Hooper. "That's what it was then." And he didn't understand what was making Blue so wild.

"I'll tell you something," whispered Blue, "but it's a secret and you can't tell anyone. Not anyone."

"Okay," said Hooper.

"I'm in love with Athena," Blue whispered, and now he looked just a bit proud.

Hooper thought about it. "In love! How can you be in love?" The idea had never crossed Hooper's mind before.

"Well, I am!" said Blue, now a bit sulky.

43

Hooper looked at Blue closely. "Hey, how old are you?"

"Twelve," said Blue. "Twelve this month."

"Oh," said Hooper. And he was still thoughtful.

"In New York," said Blue, the guide . . . Blue, the authority, "in New York, when you're twelve, you can be in love if you want to." And then he added, "But don't forget, it's a secret."

They had skated quite a while and found themselves out of their usual skating area.

"And this," Blue said, as they skated along, "is the outskirts of the Central Park Zoo—a really great place."

It was so early in the morning that almost no one was about. "Oh, let's go in," said Hooper.

"Okay," said Blue, "I'll show you some of the best things. Do you like bears?"

"I don't know," said Hooper. It turned out that he neither liked nor disliked bears. They did not arouse strong feelings in him. These were polar bears who moved slowly about on some rocks and, despite the water in the pool, managed to look like dirty rugs. Moreover, they did not seem particularly interested in Hooper and Blue.

The elephants were a different matter. They had a more outgoing nature. Their tiny eyes were alight with interest, and they regarded Blue and Hooper intently and intelligently, curling and uncurling their trunks, reaching

44

out through the bars and making friendly overtures. Hooper was delighted with them. "Now *there's* a good animal!" he said.

Blue said, "They're all right, but I don't like the color."

Hooper looked, but the elephant, despite this shortcoming, seemed very splendid. "I'll show you something I really like," said Blue. "Come on."

So they skated around the corner, past the cages where keepers were sweeping and feeding, and animals were getting ready for a busy day of being forever on stage.

"There," said Blue, and pointed up to the top of a giraffe. "Look at that face."

Hooper looked. The giraffe was quite attractive. In the first place, the coloring was a rich golden-chestnut and brown in handsome patterns. The face was a wise-looking triangle. The legs, like stilts, and incredibly long neck made this giraffe nearly as high as a two-story building. There were other giraffes in the pen and two of them seemed to be playing a game of hopscotch.

"What d'ya think?" asked Blue.

"Great!" said Hooper, to Blue's evident satisfaction. "They are great."

"Okay," said Blue, "Now look at the eyes. Look at the eyelashes." Hooper looked. "What d'ya think the eyes look like, huh?" Blue asked urgently. "Don't they make you think of . . . *someone?*"

"You don't *mean* . . . ?"

"Right!" whispered Blue. "Don't you *really* think the giraffe looks something like Athena? Come on. Tell the truth."

Hooper squinted. It was not impossible, if you looked at it a certain way, to see a slight resemblance.

"She's prettier," said Hooper.

Blue gave Hooper a look of approval and said, "Now watch when she eats."

A guard walked by, leading a goat, and said, "No skating in the zoo, boys." So they sat on the grass, loosened their skates, took off their jackets, and lay back to watch.

After a while the tallest giraffe reached her head up to a small tree and began her lunch. From under her long upper lip she whipped out the longest tongue Hooper had ever seen and began to tear small green leaves and twig tidbits from the tree. It was haughty and elegant—ladylike.

"Oh," Blue said wistfully, "I wish I could climb up there and just get a good, close look at those eyes. Look at those lashes! Just look at those lashes." They really were astounding. Hooper thought they were more astounding than Athena's, but he did not tell Blue that.

"Oh, there should be some way to get up there and look, if you want to so much," said Hooper. "Could you climb the tree?" He sat up.

"I've thought of that," said Blue, "but look, they cut off all the low branches."

"How about the wire of the cage?" asked Hooper,

going over to examine it while Blue remained staring up at the tree. "Could you get your toes in there?"

"The holes are too small," called Blue.

"If we only had a rope," said Hooper, "I think we could . . . Now if we took a rope and made a sort of noose and . . ." His eyes traveled up to the tree branches overhead, and then through the green leaves to the sky —high, blue, beautiful. The problem of Blue and the giraffe was interrupted by a skywriting airplane. It wrote USE ZANG, and then ZANG softly spread out into a white cloud. Then the airplane wrote it again. ZANG went the airplane; poof went the cloud. Over and over again.

At first Hooper didn't notice, but by the time he realized it, he had actually skimmed up a good five feet, and Blue, looking like an exclamation point, had noticed it, too.

"Hey!" was all Blue could say at first. "Hey!"

"Oh, blast!" said Hooper. "I forgot to put my coat and skates back on."

"What is it! What's happening?" asked Blue. "What are you *doing*?" Hey!" he said. "You're not a yogi are you?"

"I'm a skimmer," said Hooper reluctantly, because now the secret was out. "I skim. I always have."

"You fly, like?" said Blue, walking all around and peering up at Hooper's feet with their extra long pants flopping around them. "How do you do it? Oh wait till the kids see this!"

"No!" exclaimed Hooper. "We're keeping it a secret."

"Oh, come on," said Blue. "You gotta tell them. This is going to surprise people. Hey!" Blue was struck with brilliance. "You're not the kid who . . . ? The *Human Fly!*"

"Listen," said Hooper, and he was skimming higher now, and his mind was moving in an unaccustomed direction. His voice became less pleasant than Hooper usually sounded. "Blue," he said coldly, "if you keep this a secret, I will keep it a secret the way you feel about Athena."

Blue paled. "But you said—"

"*This* is what I'm saying now," said Hooper.

Blue looked sullen, but only for a minute. A new idea hit him. "How do you get down?" he asked.

"I wait," said Hooper.

"Well, as long as you're up there, look at her eyes. Look at her eyes," begged Blue. Hooper looked. The giraffe flicked her eyelashes, looked down with sweet curiosity, but eventually got bored and walked away.

"Very nice," said Hooper, "but I don't think it's worth the trouble to you. Forget it."

"I want you for my basketball team," said Blue as they waited. "That's part of the deal. Okay?"

"Okay," said Hooper, "But I don't play basketball."

"You will," said Blue.

The zoo guard walked by, leading the goat back. He

"Look at her eyes," begged Blue.

said, "You boys get off that fence or I'll call the cops," and walked on.

In a half hour, Hooper had got down far enough for Blue to help him fasten his skates to his shoes and hand him his jacket. In another few minutes he was down. "Phew!" he said. "That was close. I could have missed lunch."

6

There was not an exact moment when Hooper began to notice a certain man in a tweed suit. It was just a slow awareness of a stocky man, round-faced, ordinary in every way except that he did keep turning up. This alone is what put Hooper on the alert. He had noticed that in New York people did not seem to keep turning up like that and, as a matter of fact, the streets were full of new people all the time, with successions of fresh faces replacing the old ones.

And then one morning when Hooper was skating with his shadow on his way to meet Blue and sail a boat in the pond, he noticed another shadow coming along at a good clip. The shadow was smoking and looked a bit like a steam locomotive. Hooper took a quick look over his shoulder and saw the tweed-suited man smoking a pipe and chugging along quite fast. Hooper put on a bit more speed and the shadow hurried a bit, too. Then Hooper

Hooper began to give it some thought.

stopped short and took another look over his shoulder—a longer one—and the man came to a sudden stop. Hooper turned and started to skate thoughtfully. He took another quick look over his shoulder. The man with the pipe wasn't there! Instead, there was a man of the very same build, wearing the very same suit, but this man was wearing a pair of dark glasses and a hat. An odd thing was happening. Smoke was pouring from the man's pocket.

Hooper acted fast. "Hey!" he shouted skating toward the man. The man chugged to a stop and threw up his arms in surprise, as Hooper swooped down on him and started to beat at his pocket.

"Your pocket's on fire! Your pocket's on fire!" Hooper cried, beating away.

"Oh, merciful heavens!" the man said, and joined Hooper in smacking at the smoking pocket. "Oh dear! Well! Well! Oh, for goodness' sakes!" were a few more of the things he had to say on the subject, but together they managed to put out the small fire. It attracted very little attention. A few people stopped to give a casual word of advice and moved on. Several people just moved out into the gutter. One lady went "Tsk! Tsk" and crossed the street.

"Well, dear now," said the man, "I've given myself dead away. Too bad." He took off the dark glasses and revealed himself to be the selfsame tweed-suited man who had been following Hooper for days. "I really am not very good at this, though I thought this was a foolproof disguise. Just a bit warm, that's all. What really tipped you off?"

"Just the thereness of you," said Hooper. "Though I couldn't be sure, of course. What really got my attention was your pocket being on fire. That was sure interesting."

The man now reached into the cooled pocket for the pipe. "I'm not a master at sleuthing," he said. "If the truth be known, I've never done it before."

"But what *are* you doing it for?" asked Hooper. They had started to move together now, down the street, Hooper skating at a casual rate and the man, a bit winded, walking slowly beside him. He smelled a bit charred.

"It's because of your levitation thing," said the man. "I'm a part-time inventor. At the moment I'm interested in, among other things, gravitational pulls and the like. I've been wanting to observe you, but I can't get anyone to talk to me on your phone. Allow me to give you my card." He rummaged through his tweed suit but didn't find a card. Then he looked through a small notebook and thought he had found it, but it was a card for an exterminator. Then he looked through his wallet and discovered that there were no cards in it nor, it seemed, any money. He looked abashed.

"Couldn't you just tell me your name then," suggested Hooper.

"Why of course," said the man. "Why not? Young people today see things so clearly. Well then, my name is John Smith. Professor John Smith."

"John Smith," said Hooper. "That's not hard to remember."

"I keep the cards," said Professor Smith, "because people tend to doubt the name. They suspect I am hiding something."

"That's odd," said Hooper. "What I have been wondering is if people in New York worry a lot about names. I have a friend who thinks Hooper is a funny name. He thinks his own name is funny and he thinks *I* think his name is funny."

"And is it?" asked Professor Smith. "And do you?"

"I didn't," said Hooper. "His name is Blue. Blue."

"Blue," said Professor Smith thoughtfully. "Hmm. Phonically it's a perfectly sound name. Lou, for instance, is a well-known name."

"Hugh," said Hooper, getting the idea. "That's my father's name."

"Sue," said Professor Smith. "No, really, there is nothing about Blue to cause suspicion or amusement—not rationally. On the other hand, it is unusual, therefore suspect. But you see, John Smith is too simple, straightforward, and *usual*."

"But if it's usual . . ." began Hooper.

"The thing about a city," said Professor Smith, "is that to blend in, it seems you must be rather usual and not too usual. Too usual is just as bad as too unusual!"

"Like me," said Hooper.

"Perhaps," said Professor Smith. "Yes, we may have something in common." Professor Smith lit his pipe then, and dropped the matches into his pocket. They fell directly through the newly burned hole and onto the pavement. Hooper picked them up and handed them to Professor Smith.

"Hm," said Professor Smith. "That hole is a hole."

Hooper had to agree, and he liked the simple and direct way that the Professor had of speaking.

They had reached the park and Hooper skated down the curved path, doing one of his fancier turns at the bottom in a shameless bit of showing off. Professor Smith did not seem terribly impressed.

"I'm going over to the sailboat pond," said Hooper. "My friend Blue is going to be there."

"May I come along?" asked Professor Smith.

"Sure," said Hooper. "You can come and watch."

"Thank you," said Professor Smith. He was a courteous person.

"How'd you know about the . . . um . . . skimming?" asked Hooper, as they made their way along the early-morning paths, fresh as country in the middle of the dusty city.

"Saw you with my own eyes," said Professor Smith. "Live right around the corner, you see. Happened to be going by the day you went into the third-floor window."

"But why follow me?" asked Hooper.

"Inventors have got to keep alert to what's going on. When I see someone with an invention that is in my field, I have to find out as much as I can. Simple as that."

"Invention?" asked Hooper.

"Your invention, in this case," said Professor Smith.

"My invention?" said Hooper. "I haven't got any invention."

"All right," said Professor Smith patiently and kindly. "I don't want to put you in any kind of embarrassing position. Probably it isn't your invention. Probably it's your father's invention or your uncle's invention, and I wouldn't want you to betray them, of course. Ethical question, that is. Just you go about your business. I'll spy as much as I can without disturbing you or putting you in a position to betray anyone, although I really don't care for this sleuthing a bit."

"But . . ." began Hooper, but the look on Professor Smith's face made Hooper know that Professor Smith had set his mind on this inventing thing and right now he was not going to be convinced that the skimming was *not* the result of some device.

They got to the sailboat pond early. Blue had not arrived. The pool was still and unrippled. Standing at the edge, Hooper and Professor Smith could see each other standing heads down in the water. Their reflections smiled at each other. Hooper had a sudden whim to put his feet in the water, so he sat at the edge of the pond and removed his skates and his shoes and socks and dipped both feet in. Professor Smith found the scene irresistible and in a moment he had his shoes and socks off too, and side by side, they sat splashing little waves and watching them move outward from the edge of the pool.

"What sort of thing do you invent?" asked Hooper. "Are you good?"

Professor Smith was thoughtful. "Yes, I'm good," he said. "But I'm not what they call successful. For instance, I have not even acquired large amounts of wealth. As to what I invent, I invent much-needed three-dimensional things, but unfortunately, in every instance, the fourth dimension has intervened to make them obsolete before their completion."

"I guess I don't understand that," said Hooper.

"The fourth dimension, in the simplest terms, is time. Time passes, and my inventions become more or less useless."

"Like how?" asked Hooper.

"Well, take the quiet horseshoe," said Professor Smith. "After years of very intensive research I invented a horseshoe of enormous durability that is absolutely quiet. A milkman's horse could go down the street at four A.M. without waking a soul."

"That's nice," said Hooper.

"Very," agreed Professor Smith. "But how many horse-drawn milk wagons do you see? And how many people do you know who are in the market for horseshoes at all—noisy or quiet?"

"None," said Hooper.

"That's it," said Professor Smith, shrugging. "The need for horseshoes has diminished to a point where no one is interested in producing my invention. Its usefulness decreases with each passing day. It has become irrelevant."

"What else?" asked Hooper.

"Well, I have an automatic shoe-buttoner."

"But I never see shoes that button," said Hooper.

"There you are!" said Professor Smith. "That's the thing. So with a history like that I have decided to devote myself to something that can't go out of date before I invent it, even if it takes forever. And that is why I have decided on"—he looked around nervously and lowered his voice—"the Smith Levitational Shoe."

"Levitational shoe," said Hooper. "Hm."

"My preliminary model is well under way, *but if you are already there ahead of me, I am not going to go on. No, I am certainly not going to get myself into another dead end. I am generally a cheerful fellow, but it is just too depressing. But of course, you understand," and Professor Smith brightened, "this is only a summertime profession."

"What are you the rest of the time?" asked Hooper.

"I'm a university professor of history," replied Professor Smith.

"Oh, history!" said Hooper, and he was just about to tell Professor Smith about the volume of H. G. Wells and especially about the chapter on the Normans, the Saracens, the Hungarians, and the Seljuk Turks, but at that moment Blue appeared around the far end of the pond carrying a sailboat, and by a wonderful coincidence

Athena and October appeared at the same moment, carrying long sticks.

Hooper got up and said, "Those are my friends. I guess I'll go over and give them a hand," and he hurried off in the direction of the little group, now busily concentrating on launching the sailboat.

Professor Smith waited until Hooper was well on his way, and then he reached over and picked up one of Hooper's shoes. He turned it over and over. It looked just like any other shoe he had ever seen.

"Hm . . ." he mused. "That's interesting. A very good job." He scratched his brow. "How could they conceal the mechanism so well? Good heavens, my idea is noth-

"My idea is nothing this slick!"

ing this slick!" He was very depressed. He looked at the sole of the shoe, then at the heel. He took out a tape measure and measured the inside and then the outside. He tapped the heel with his pencil. For a moment he thought he detected something suspicious, but a second tap revealed that the rattle was in the pencil. Professor Smith shook his head in pure wonderment. "Astounding. There is absolutely nothing levitational about this shoe!"

He turned his attention to Hooper and the others who had now launched the ship which was sailing, but lazily, around the perimeter of the pond. There really wasn't much of a breeze.

"There's not enough wind," Blue said. "It's just not a good day for it. Let's get the boat back and go do something else." He reached out with his stick and started to guide the boat to the pond's edge, but the boat slipped away and sailed just a bit farther out. "Ah," he said, "it's just out of reach. I'll have to wait until it comes in a bit more." But the boat seemed to be going out.

"Here, let me try," said Hooper. "My arms are longer." He took the stick and reached out. He didn't quite make it. Then he reached some more, and some more, and before anyone had noticed it, even Hooper himself, he was skimming out at his normal height, over the pond, dragging his trouser cuffs in the water. "Got it!" he said, and started guiding the boat back to the shore. And then he noticed the eyes of his friends, and the mouths of his friends, and out of the corner of his eye he saw Professor Smith running toward them, and then from

61

behind a bush there was a flash of light and the rush of someone running off. October screamed and Athena kept saying, "Hey! Hey!" Hooper said, "Oh, blast!" and skimmed back to shore and sat down and, for the first time in his life, sulked. Blue, of course, was silent and kept looking sideways at Hooper.

"All right," Hooper said. "All right. Now you know. So take a good look! I'm a skimmer. I skim. I've always skimmed. I never minded it one bit. I never even cared one way or the other. And just for a while it looked like there might be some . . . well, never mind. But now . . . gosh, I am just plain sick of all this sneaking about. So there you are, take it or leave it. That's the way it is."

Professor Smith arrived at that point, and he said, "Boy! My boy! Where is it, then? Not in the shoes. Where is it?"

"Nowhere," said Hooper, now thoroughly annoyed. "Nowhere. It's nowhere. Just in me. I do not have an invention. I do not have a patent. I do not have anything except just the way I am." And he got up to go. He started skimming briskly around the circumference of the pond, followed at a clip by Professor Smith, Blue, Athena, and October, in that order.

"Don't go, Hooper," cried Professor Smith. "I want to talk with you."

"Don't go, Hooper," yelled Blue. "You don't have to be sore." Athena and October, being ladylike, did not yell, but they ran like anything to keep up.

Hooper got to the place where he had left his shoes

and socks and skates and sat down to put them on. He felt very strange. "What's the matter with me?" he asked himself. "What am I so mad about?"

"What are you so mad about?" asked Blue, coming to sit beside him.

"I don't know," said Hooper. "I just don't know."

"Ah ha!" said Professor Smith. "Let me ask you this. If you had a choice, would you choose to skim?"

Hooper looked confused.

"I realize that is a highly personal question and don't feel you have to answer it," said Professor Smith. "But, if you wish, give it some thought. It might possibly help me with my invention. Think it over and come and see me. Here's my card." And he went through his pocket and wallet and found no card.

"Why don't you just tell me where you live?" said Hooper.

"Oh, good boy!" exclaimed Professor Smith. "Well, then. Right around the corner from you. First building on the right. Basement floor, and there you are." And he turned on his heel and was off.

"What a batty old man," said Blue.

"No he's not," said Hooper. "He's not a bit batty, and he's very nice. He's an inventor."

"What does he invent?" asked October.

"Oh, different things that do different things," said Hooper.

"Oh," said October.

"Well, let's all go over and see his inventions, then,"

said Blue. "Let's go tomorrow, or the next day, or the next day, or pretty soon. Okay?"

"Okay," said Hooper. And everyone else agreed that that was a good idea. Hooper got up and started skating up the path and they all followed. October hurried a little to walk beside him. She gave him a smile, but Hooper didn't notice. *Something* was bothering him and he didn't know just what it was.

7

"And I don't know what it is." Hooper had been talking to Professor Smith for an hour, and now he was winding up a long recital of events that had led to this minute. It included what he remembered of his young life in East Westham, his various attacks, the move to New York, the hubbub and excitement, the hiding and the fuss—all the things building up in his mind—and now this new *feeling*. Everything came tumbling out. He took a long drink of something cold and refreshingly sour that Professor Smith gave him in an icy glass.

It was while Hooper had been making his way from the sailboat pond back to his apartment that he got the idea of not going straight home. He cruised around and around for a while, skating unobtrusively up one street and down another, thinking and thinking. And then he found himself in front of Professor Smith's apartment house, and remembering the very recent invitation to call, Hooper left his skates at the door, and called.

Professor Smith was attentive and interested, offering only an occasional nod, a brief question, a smile or a frown. But now that Hooper seemed to have finished his story, Professor Smith took a deep breath, tucked his chin down into his neck, and spoke quietly.

"What is it that seems to bother you most?" he asked.

"Well, the hiding, I guess, and the feeling that . . . that . . . just something is wrong."

"That you are supposed to be some other way?" suggested Professor Smith.

"Yes, I think so," admitted Hooper.

"Pressure," Professor Smith said solemnly. "The pressure of society." Hooper looked interested. It was not only interesting, but it made him feel very important to be discussed so seriously. "Now as I see it," Professor Smith went on, "up until now—that is, when you were in East Westham—you were perfectly happy with yourself as you were."

"Everything was fine," said Hooper.

"Now, suddenly, many things and many people seem strange to you, and they look upon you as strange. It seems to be necessary to hide a very important side of yourself—the skimming—one of the things that makes you you."

"Yes," Hooper interrupted in a rush, "and when I have to hide that way, it makes me feel . . . it makes me feel . . ."

"Undesirable?" suggested Professor Smith.

"I guess so," Hooper said.

66

"Whereas, before, skimming had been neither desirable nor undesirable . . . just there."

Hooper was nodding. Some of the things Professor Smith said made wonderful sense. They really did.

"Then perhaps you don't want to be different?"

"I don't know," said Hooper. "I do and I don't."

"Well, then," Professor Smith went on, "maybe *that's* what could be bothering you. Do you think so?"

"What?" asked Hooper.

"Just the question of whether you *want* to be as you are. 'Do I like myself the way I am?' 'Will people like me the way I am?' Maybe this is the reason you are feeling discontented. Mind you, we have only just met, and I am only guessing at this. I could be all wrong. I often am."

"No," Hooper said. "You could be right. It *feels* like what's bothering me, when you say it."

"Discontent is not one of the feelings you are used to managing."

Hooper nodded. "There's just this one other thing, though," he said. "It's that ever since that day—the day I went up the building wall to open the window . . ."

"The day the beans were spilled, eh?"

"Yes, ever since then, I keep having this idea that . . . well, there were all these phone calls, you know, offering me lots of things . . . well, you know . . . and I think maybe . . ."

"Visions of wide notoriety?" suggested Professor Smith.

Hooper nodded. "And . . ."

"The intriguing rattle of money? The profit motive!"

Hooper felt suddenly as though he had finally found on his arm the exact spot that was itching and was able to scratch it. He smiled at Professor Smith and got up to leave. He felt quite good, for no reason that he could find, and despite the fact that Professor Smith offered him no ideas or cures, no instant remedies for troubles, no directions as to what to do.

But before Hooper could leave, Professor Smith hurriedly rummaged about and brought out the nearly completed model of the levitational shoe. "Well, what do you think of it?" he asked. "Don't be afraid. Say what you think." It appeared to be based mainly on one of a pair of galoshes.

"It's quite big," Hooper ventured.

"To accommodate the machinery," said Professor Smith. "We'd have to refine the appearance, if it's a fashion matter, but that seems secondary. Still, I suppose people will want to look chic even when flying. So, yes, I suppose you're right. I should consider its appearance."

"Perhaps with buttons," suggested Hooper. "Then you'd have a use for the automatic buttonhook."

"My word!" said Professor Smith with genuine admiration in his voice. "You are an exceptionally astute young man."

Hooper was pleased. So he went on. "How does it work?"

"It doesn't," replied Professor Smith. "That's its only

"It's quite big," Hooper ventured.

other major drawback. But on the drawing board it is a success, and it is only a matter of time before I perfect it. It's a question of time only. And you see, in the winter, when I am surrounded by students, I am not inclined to give much time to this sort of thing. As I explained, it is a summertime job with me. However, since I can see you offer no competition, I am really glad you came by. You've encouraged me to continue my work, even if it takes years. You have helped me immeasurably."

"You've helped me, too," said Hooper.

"Now, in that connection," began Professor Smith, whipping out a notebook and starting to nibble a pencil thoughtfully, "it has crossed my mind that perhaps, before you go, you might like to try a little experiment."

"Okay," said Hooper. "What sort of experiment?"

"Well, since you've just told me a bit about your skimming attacks in East Westham, I though we might try to analyze a more recent one—one you could remember more clearly. To begin with, do you think you could remember *just* what you were *doing* that day you went up the side of the apartment building? Were you in any special *position*, for instance? How were you standing? Were you standing or sitting, in fact? What position were your feet in? Your arms? Your head?"

"Well, let's see," said Hooper, thinking back. "I know I was standing or . . ." he blushed a bit. "You know . . . skimming, like always."

"Of course," said Professor Smith. "That's understood. Go on."

"I don't remember anything special. I was just looking up at the windows and wondering how to get into the apartment . . . and then I skimmed up above my father's head."

"So your head was up!" said Professor Smith. "Aha!" and he wrote in his little notebook: *Position of head.* "And then what?" he asked.

"Then I just stayed there. And then, oh yes, my father asked me a riddle to entertain me while I waited to come down. And while I was thinking about it," Hooper laughed, "I skimmed up some more. And then I climbed in the window. And that's all."

Professor Smith, though a jolly man, had not joined in Hooper's laughter. From the look on his face, you might believe he had stopped listening and was half-asleep. He wasn't. "A riddle," he said thoughtfully. And then suddenly he snapped, "Go stand over there!" But then he softened his tone. "Excuse me," he said. "I tend to get a bit bossy when I am working."

"Oh, that's all right," said Hooper generously, though actually he had been surprised by the sudden change in Professor Smith. He skimmed over to the spot the Professor had pointed to—a relatively clear place in the center of the cluttered room.

"Now, try and get yourself in the position you were in that day," said Professor Smith. Hooper tried, but he couldn't remember that there had been anything special about it.

"Now look up." Hooper looked up. It was an unusual

sight, actually. Professor Smith's apartment was in the basement of the building and the ceiling was woven with many pipes that presumably carried hot and cold water to all parts of the building. Slung from the pipes were baskets of all sizes and pots of all dimensions, some holding papers, plants, bric-a-brac, all but spilling out of their containers. Hooper looked at them with fascination. One bright red raffia basket, right over the middle of the room, was tightly covered. It had a chain with a lock on it. Hooper wondered what was in it.

"Now," said Professor Smith, "I am going to give you a riddle."

"A riddle!" exclaimed Hooper. "What kind of scientific experiment is that?"

"We are trying to re-create, in the laboratory, so to speak, the situation you just described," Professor Smith said. "Now, are you ready?"

"Ready," said Hooper.

"Listen carefully, then. Let us say that a sweater, worn in the usual way, has a label on the inside of the collar. Assuming that the sleeve which accommodates the left arm when the sweater is worn normally is referred to as the left sleeve, where will the label be if the sweater is turned inside out, and the right arm is put into the left sleeve and the left arm is put into the right sleeve? Will the label be on the front outside? On the front inside? Back inside? Back outside?"

There was complete silence in the room. Hooper had

never done a problem like that before. Now let's see. In his mind Hooper started to slip his left arm out of the imaginary sweater and turn it inside out. That would put the back of the sweater in front, wouldn't it? Or would it? Now, in his mind, he tried putting his right arm into the sleeve. No, that was wrong. He was badly mixed up. He stared up at the covered red basket overhead, but its bright sides offered him no help. What in the world could be in that basket, anyway . . . all chained up? Nothing could be seen spilling out, like the other baskets. It was deep and quite strong. Perhaps it held something like a rare vicious snake. It would be a pretty good place to keep a snake . . .

"Okay!" cried the Professor. "What's the answer?"

Answer! Hooper suddenly realized that he had forgotten the question—and he was a good four feet off the floor! He made a guess. "Front inside," he said.

"Wrong!" cried Professor Smith, with seeming delight. "You got the wrong answer and skimmed up anyway."

"Hey!" cried Hooper, looking down. "You mean, just *doing* riddles makes me skim higher!"

"Perhaps, but *only* perhaps," said Professor Smith. "That may be putting it too simply. But there may be *something* there that is related to it—just how, or in what ratio, is more than I can measure at this time. It gives us something to work on, though. Now don't worry about it a bit. Just relax and carry on as usual."

73

"I'll have to come down first," said Hooper.

"Oh dear!" said Professor Smith. "What do you usually do about that?"

"I'm not so awfully high," said Hooper. "Maybe if you put my skates on me, I could manage."

Hooper's idea worked, and the Professor added a couple of heavy books to complete the job. Hooper started out the door carrying the books. "That was interesting," he said to Professor Smith. But the Professor was already seated at his desk, writing furiously in his notebook. He did not seem to hear Hooper's good-bye.

When Hooper returned home to the apartment it was midafternoon and he knew at once that something was out of the ordinary. His father was home. His father was never home at this time of day unless it was a national holiday. It was not a national holiday, therefore Hooper suspected that something was out of the ordinary. It was. Mrs. Toote was sitting with the early edition of the evening newspaper open on her lap. There was a picture of Hooper on the front page—a great big picture of Hooper skimming over the Central Park pond. Mrs. Toote was sniffling.

Mr. Toote was on the telephone. He was being very controlled, but with difficulty. "Give me your name, address, and details of your offer," he said. "I'm making a list. We'll think about it. That's all I can tell you at this time." He listened for a moment, wrote something on what seemed to be a considerable list, and hung up. "Whoosh!" he said. Or something like that.

Hooper looked over his mother's shoulder at the story in the paper. " 'What Makes Hooper Fly?' " he read aloud. "How do they know my name?"

"Snooping!" explained Mrs. Toote, with heat. "Just plain, old-fashioned, country variety snooping."

The story went on to explain that "this newspaper's go-getter photographer had been following the suspect for days and had finally caught him in the very act of flying."

"Now that sneaky man with the camera is their 'go-getter photographer'!" Mrs. Toote observed.

"Aw, I don't fly," said Hooper. "Can't that fellow see I'm just skimming?"

"Sometimes newspapers exaggerate," said Mr. Toote. "They do it to make things more exciting. *Fly* will probably sell more papers than *skim*. All right, now we have got to look this thing right in the eye. The cat's out of the bag. The news is out. The lid's off the box, and we might as well call a spade a spade and get down to brass tacks."

"Oh, Hugh!" said Mrs. Toote. "Just talk straight out."

"Right," said Mr. Toote. "The question is just this— will it do any harm to look into these offers? That's what I am asking myself."

"Hugh!" cried Mrs. Toote. "Anyhow, Hooper doesn't do *tricks*."

75

"Just *look*, mind you, and see what's what. Listen to reason, then think it over."

"How can that hurt anything, Mum?" asked Hooper. "Just look and listen and see what everybody really wants. Maybe we can make a million; right, Pop?" Somehow he wasn't feeling mixed up or worried anymore.

Mr. Toote bit his bottom lip. "A million," he said, "more or less."

Mrs. Toote looked up. "A million!" she exclaimed. "Oh dear! Oh, Hooper! Oh, Hugh!" And then she was crying again. "Honestly, I wish we were back in East Westham."

Hooper put his arm around his mother. "Listen," he said, "let Pop see what it is they all want. Then if you don't want it, we won't do it. Right, Pop?"

"Right," said Mr. Toote.

"Well, all right then," said Mrs. Toote. "I guess I do have to keep an open mind. But don't sign anything, Hugh."

"Okay," said Mr. Toote, "I won't even sign a check for your household allowance this week, my dear." And he laughed and clapped his son on the back.

Hooper received the clap with an absentminded chuckle. He was reading the article in the newspaper from start to finish. Actually, it was the first time he had ever read an entire newspaper article, though he sometimes read the headlines and the sports results. He went on to read the article below it. It was about a bunch of people, right here in this city, who got together and went

76

down to City Hall to find the mayor and tell him what they thought about the way things were going in the city. They didn't think things were going so well, it seems. They had a hard time getting in touch with the mayor, and there seemed to be some kind of fight about it. It was a really interesting story. He wanted to find out how it came out so he turned to page thirty-seven, where it was continued. There were a bunch of pictures of some of the people, so that made it even more interesting—like a real book sort of story. It was as interesting as some of the chapters in H. G. Wells. He wondered if it would be continued the next day, like the comics.

Under that was a little story about an island called Aitutaki. He was settling down to read the story because the name sounded good, when Mr. Toote saw the pile of books Hooper had set down on the table. "Been to the library, son?" Mr. Toote asked, picking up one of the books—*The History of Everyday Things*.

"No," said Hooper. "A really keen man lent them to me—a guy I met."

"What man?" asked Mrs. Toote anxiously. "You mustn't befriend just *anyone* in the city, Hooper."

"Oh, Professor Smith isn't just anyone," Hooper said a bit proudly. "He's a real professor at the University, and he's an inventor, and he's very nice besides. You'd like him."

"In that case, we must meet him," said Mrs. Toote, back to her usual hospitable self. "We must have him over for tea some afternoon."

"Okay," said Hooper, getting back to the business of finding what else was hidden in the pages of the newspaper.

After dinner that evening Hooper thought about Professor Smith's riddle. He also thought about the red raffia basket with the chain on it. But there was no way of guessing what was in the basket so he went back to the riddle.

As Hooper was going off to bed, Mrs. Toote said, "Hooper, I do believe your sweater is inside out. Have you been wearing it that way all day?"

"No," Hooper said. "Just since now."

8

Mr. Toote arranged a leave of absence from his job and dedicated himself in the next several weeks to the investigation of offers, the details of which made his mind boggle. But one thing at a time, he kept reminding himself.

Hooper worked up several interesting disguises—an extra-long raincoat, a motorcycle helmet, a pogo stick (a very good disguise, this was), and he made a sort of game of never looking the same twice, and this took some of the discomfort out of the hiding. In this way he was successful in evading gawking, rubbernecking reporters and the countless small children who now came in response to the continued newspaper publicity. Some of the children had been trying their own luck skimming the pond and had to be fished out by the annoyed park custodians. A few had even tried jumping from heights and had received minor injuries. The Tootes felt very bad about that.

Hooper worked up several interesting disguises.

For Hooper, life kept whizzing right along, and "pretty soon"—the day the children had decided to pay a visit to Professor Smith—arrived. Hooper hurried to the park to meet his friends, wearing one of his better disguises, a skin-diving suit that had been given to him as a going-away present by his Uncle Matt, the one with the scientific turn of mind. He knew New York was near the ocean and he was interested to know if a skimmer might have a different experience skin diving than a non-skimmer. As yet, Hooper had not had the chance to find out. Meanwhile the mask was a very good face disguise, but the suit was quite hot. What with the hurrying and the heat, Hooper arrived in the park early, overheated and out of breath. He decided to sit on one of the benches near the path and wait for Blue, Athena, and October. He wished they'd hurry. He was awfully eager for them to really get to know his interesting new acquaintance, the Professor.

Strangely, nearly all the benches were occupied. On them, sitting quietly, were mostly sad-looking old men in dark, thready clothes, staring with no brightness at all at the bright world around them. Who are they? Hooper asked himself. He had never noticed them before. Had they been there all the time? One old man got up and started a shuffling walk down the path. Hooper went to the seat the man had vacated and hesitated just a minute before he sat down beside the scruffy-looking man now sitting there alone. Suddenly the man dove under the bench to pick up something. He came up with a peanut. He had reached it before the squirrel who was scrambling for it. The man cracked the peanut solemnly and crunched it with some difficulty with his intermittent teeth. He looked at Hooper with no embarrassment. Even so, for some reason Hooper felt himself an intruder. He bent over to tighten his skates. The man spotted another peanut and their heads were down under the bench at about the same moment. "Deep-sea divin'?" asked the man, giving Hooper a Halloweenish sort of smile. Hooper, for reasons he did not know, got up without answering and, as quickly as he could, he skated up the path. He ran into Blue, Athena, and October on the way.

"Okay, let's go!" said Hooper.

"What's the rush?" asked Blue.

Hooper looked over his shoulder. The man was ducking down for another peanut. A feeling came over Hooper that got between him and the plan for the morning. *I didn't answer him,* he thought to himself. *I didn't say hello, and I didn't say good-bye.* And there was something else. What was it? He pushed the thoughts to the back of his mind. "We don't want to be late," he said.

On the way over he told the others something about Professor Smith's interesting inventions. "They're sort of top secret," said Hooper. "Maybe he will show them to you, if you ask."

"Did he show them to you?" asked Blue.

"Yes," Hooper said.

"Then he'll show them to me," said Blue.

There was an elaborate black iron fence in front of the old brownstone house, and Hooper led them around it and down the short flight of stairs to the basement. They knocked on the door . . . knocked again . . . and after what seemed a very long time, Professor Smith appeared. He was wearing a tennis cap with a green eyeshade, a long gray cardigan sweater, and a pair of substantial hiking boots. The boots made a good firm thumping noise as he approached the door. He threw it wide and gave them a very nice welcome.

"Friends, friends, friends!" he said. "Come in, come in, come in." They trooped in, having to be very careful where they put their feet because the apartment floor was carpeted deeply with nearly everything Professor Smith possessed—stacks of newspapers, stacks of closely written looseleaf paper, several piles of assorted clothing, a great many measuring tapes, odd-looking instruments, pencils, slide rules, compasses, rulers, and scales.

A ship's hammock was slung in one corner of the room, and into this Professor Smith now climbed. It folded itself around him like friendly arms and very little of Professor Smith remained to be seen except his cheerful face. The children peered at him. "Sit down, sit down," he said, indicating the floor. "This is my working corner. In the absence of inspiration, I have a splendid view, through that window, of many feet going by. I often wonder where they are going."

Hooper looked around for signs of work, but the general clutter made it hard to focus on anything in particular. "What are you working on right now?" Hooper asked.

"Thinking, mostly," said Professor Smith. "This is really the thinking part of the room, and," he added, "though it may appear to you to be slightly disarranged, it is actually a very well-ordered household. That pile of books over there, for instance, relates to the subject on which I am now at work. That stack of papers, a little to the east of it, are papers relating to my original thinking on the problem. The stack of books, just beyond, are books that are supposed to be returned to the library. And so forth."

"What about the thumbtacks all over the floor?" asked October.

"Ah," replied Professor Smith. "They're not entirely without a reason. They're to remind me not to go barefoot. Catch cold that way, you know."

"What sort of thinking are you doing?" asked Hooper.

"Well, right now, I am doing research on some of the things about modern civilization that will confuse, delude, misinform, and generally mix up the people and historians of the future."

"What did he say?" October asked softly.

Hooper said, "I *think* he means that some things we do now are going to look sort of funny later on."

"Right," said Professor Smith. October looked admiringly at Hooper, and Hooper, surprisingly, blushed. "That's it in a nutshell," the Professor continued. "Some very simple things may *seem* to be one thing when they are really something else, unless we make accurate historical records and statements. In a few hundred or thousand years, people may have a hard time figuring out some very ordinary things about us, as we are right now."

"Like what?" asked Blue.

"Well, just one example... In the back of many medicine cabinets you will notice a very small slot..."

"That's for razor blades," said Athena. "I know. I see my father drop the used razor blades down that slot so they won't be around to cut yourself on."

"That's right," said Professor Smith. "That's right. And what do you think happens to those razor blades? I'll tell you what happens. They fall down into the walls, down into the foundations, and thousands and thousands

84

of houses and other buildings of this great modern nation are absolutely stacked with rusted razor blades. Now, what do you suppose future archaeologists and historians will think, excavating old ruins, old foundations, and finding them full of rusty razor blades, long after the need, perhaps, for razor blades has disappeared? Won't they think it odd—a concentration of razor blades like that—rusted, stacked, mounded? Will it seem to be some strange ceremonial rite, that after shaving the face, the people of our time stacked their razor blades as memorials in their cellars?"

"Or maybe," suggested Hooper, "they might think we were very small people and those were our swords, like."

"That's it!" said Professor Smith. "That's it, exactly. The confusion we cause by overlooking simple things. And it's just that sort of thing that I want to clear up. Nothing must be left to guesswork, unless it has to be."

Hooper was thumbing through one of the books in a nearby stack There was a picture of a butcher's bill that was more than four thousand years old. It was not written on paper like the butcher's bills that came to Hooper's house, but it was carved in clay in a very strange writing. "Things like this?" he asked. "This is the sort of thing you have to know about?"

"Right," said Professor Smith. "Things like that. In this case, first, we have to be able to read the language. Then we have to know that it is indeed a butcher's bill and not, oh, let us say, an abstract work of art. So you see, that's an idea of the sort of thing I do, in part at least. Actually, what I am is a thinker, but there is very little market for pure thought." He sighed a bit sadly. "Thinking needs to be transformed into marketable goods in order to produce loot. A sorry state, but that is why I do a little moonlighting in the summer and produce my inventions. That way I can be even more useful to humanity and, at the same time, possibly make a little extra . . . um . . . loot."

"But what do you need the loot for?" asked Hooper. You seem to have everything you need." He looked admiringly around the homey-looking mess. The piles of odds and ends seemed familiar and rather comfortable, warming the room with their lively disorder and even making it exciting, when you thought of what the stacks contained.

"Well, loot is a confusing thing about our society," said Professor Smith. "I feel, of course, it cannot be the *most* important thing—that is, to earn money so that you can *just* have money is nothing . . . to me. But I do admit that even a man who lives as simply as I do finds that a certain amount of loot leaves him free to do other things."

And then, at the request of Blue, who had been impatient to get to the "top secret" inventions, Professor Smith brought out, without urging, the silent horseshoe. It took a while to find, but it was being used to hold down a stack of unpaid bills and the Professor found it after he thought about it for a while.

Though the children were polite, they didn't see too

much to cheer about in it. Blue, especially, was disappointed. He liked the automatic buttonhook, though, and Professor Smith had an old pair of button shoes on which he demonstrated its usefulness.

"That's a shame," said Hooper. "A good thing like that, going to waste."

"Fashion being what it is today," said the cheerful Professor, "it looks like button shoes may return to vogue, and I will be that much ahead of the times."

"I could make this place very tidy," said October, looking around. "I could sweep it . . . "

"We could all help you get it . . . well . . . cleaned up," said Athena.

"Cleaned up?" said Professor Smith, looking around to see if this were actually something that needed doing. "Well, yes, I suppose it could stand a bit of spring cleaning."

"Summer cleaning," said October.

"Well, I'd be grateful for the help," said Professor Smith. "How about a day next week?"

They all pondered the days of next week and decided that Thursday sounded like a nice, neutral, middle-of-the-week kind of day.

Hooper was still thumbing through the book he had picked up on archaeological artifacts, so Professor Smith said, "If you want to, you may borrow the book and bring it back next visit. Here's another that you might like." And before he left, Hooper saw four books he liked —one on ancient history, one on modern history, one on

English history, and one on archaeological artifacts. It was too hard to choose, so Professor Smith said to take them all. The weight of them, plus the calibrated weights and his roller skates, made Hooper feel more strongly in touch with the ground than he was accustomed to feeling. The sense of ground beneath him was still quite strange. *But*, thought Hooper, *I think I am getting used to feeling strange.*

9

"How about a skate to the zoo?" called Blue, whipping into the park that next Thursday and finding Hooper lying on the grass. Blue had taken to wearing disguises now, just for the fun of it. Even Hooper had trouble recognizing him as he approached in a fringed leather jacket, white gloves, and top hat.

"I'll see you later at Professor Smith's," Hooper called back, keeping his place in one of the Professor's books. "I'm nearly through with this Hundred Years' War."

"A hundred years is a long time," said Blue. Hooper began to think so, too, so he skipped ahead to Richard III, a very peculiar, mean king. How could they have a king like that! But for years after that, Hooper kept meaning to go back and find out how the Hundred Years' War turned out.

Later, a bit eye-weary and hot from reading in the bright sun, he began to feel the pangs of hunger he

Blue had taken to wearing disguises now.

usually got while reading. He decided to stop at the shady bench near the path and eat the apple he kept for just such an emergency. He gathered up his books, skated over, and found that the same old man he had met once before was seated there. Was he there again . . . or still? And was he the same man? There were so many. But yes, this man was now diving down under the bench. Another peanut! Once more beating the squirrel to it.

Hooper sat down, but he thought, *he doesn't recognize me because I'm not wearing my skin-diving suit.* The knowledge made him feel better for some reason. And now he said "Hello" to the man. The man turned his head slowly and, at first, only stared at Hooper. Then, slowly, he gave him that same pumpkin-like smile. Then the man dived down under the bench again. Hooper looked around as he rested and cooled off. The park was full of the usual bright boys and girls, bright kites dipping in blue skies over green grass, zoo balloons bobbing and diving above shouting children. The world of the park! But here on the bench the sunlight broke into dappled bits. It fell on the old men in shadows.

Hooper reached into his pocket for the apple and was about to lift it to his mouth when a thought or feeling caught him somewhere between his head and his belly. The apple stayed in his hand, close to his pocket. Then, quietly, Hooper released his hold on the apple and set it, unnoticed, on the seat between himself and the old man. He said a quick "Bye" and started hurriedly on his way to Professor Smith's. At the top of the path he looked back. The man was eating the apple. Another feeling came over Hooper. It was a familiar, heady feeling, almost like . . . almost like . . . No, he couldn't quite say what it was.

"You're sure stirring up this city, Hooper," said Blue, when Hooper skated into Professor Smith's apartment a little late.

"I know," said Hooper, as he set about helping them tidy up and sort several boxes of archaeological artifacts, under Professor Smith's direction.

"How are you feeling about all that attention now, my friend?" asked Professor Smith, as he examined an artifact under a magnifying glass. He discarded it. "That's an old broken collar button of mine," he said. "It somehow got in with some Egyptian relics. That's the sort of thing to throw doubt on an entire collection."

"The attention . . . " began Hooper. "Well, I don't

mind it so much anymore, although I am very good at these disguises so that people don't recognize me on the street, but—I don't care so much if they do now. I don't know why." Professor Smith smiled. "All the same," Hooper continued, "the phone rings a lot with all these offers, and it makes me feel sort of . . . important."

"Well, that's all right," said Professor Smith. "We all like to feel important, some way or other. Still, you mustn't feel . . ." he hesitated. "You mustn't think this is the *only* way you could ever feel important."

Hooper thought about it.

The girls swept and dusted, and Hooper and Blue were very useful helping the Professor sort the historical materials. While they sorted, Hooper told Professor Smith about some of the things that had interested him most in the books he had borrowed.

"Listen!" Hooper said. "That Hundred Years' War . . . there was this terrible mix-up, see. One king kept grabbing the crown away from the next guy. And it kept going on that way." He did not admit that he had skipped ahead when it had gone on a bit too long. A hundred years! "And now I'm reading about this king, Richard the Third. How could they have a king like that?" Professor Smith turned around and gave Hooper a questioning look.

"Like what?" he asked.

"Like he was a really scary sort of king," Hooper said. "He was very ugly and mean and he took these two little princes—just little kids—and he locked them in the Tower of London and then he had them *killed!*"

Professor Smith stopped his work for a minute. "That's a long and muddled story," he said. "*Muddled* . . . that's the point. Remember it. Actually, history does tell it that way, but there are some people, even today, who think old Richard was betrayed and slandered and that the stories about him are not true." The Professor shrugged. "*There's* the problem. As for the Hundred Years' War—a terrible mix-up, you say. And that . . ." and he seemed to say it sadly, ". . . that was just a *hundred* years."

"*Just* a hundred years!" Hooper exclaimed. He wanted to talk more about it, but Professor Smith was back to the matter at hand—the enormous boxes of what looked to Hooper like junk.

"All right, now," said Professor Smith, viewing them with satisfaction. "These are all marvelously organized." He surveyed the well-sorted bits of rusted tools, fragmented pottery, and slivers of this and that. "A workman who lived only to serve the Emperor Cheops may have made that bowl." He picked up an orangey fragment. "Almost five thousand years ago."

"Five thousand years!" Hooper said. "Well, *that was* a long time. Wasn't it?"

"Well," Professor Smith thought it over. "It's fifty times longer than a hundred years." Hooper did the sum in his head and had to agree it was the right answer, but it was not exactly the kind of answer he was looking for.

"Now let me see," Professor Smith said, coming back to the present. "Where shall we store these old manuscripts?"

"There's an empty space on that shelf way up there," said Blue. "I'll bet Hooper could get up there easy, if he wanted to." Blue took a great deal of personal pride in Hooper's abilities.

"Hooper," said Professor Smith, "would you want to try and take up this load?" He was looking at Hooper as if there were a special meaning to the question.

"I don't know . . ." Hooper was a little confused. "I don't usually *try* to skim up high, you know. *You* know," he said again.

"I know," said Professor Smith, "But I thought perhaps you might like to continue testing along the lines we started a few days ago. Would you?"

"Okay," said Hooper, looking just a bit nervously at his friends.

"Testing what?" asked Blue.

"We're testing a theory . . . or, at least, trying to build a theory to test," said Professor Smith. "If you like, you may have the privilege of watching." Hooper felt better. After all, if it was a privilege to watch Professor Smith at work, it was even more of a privilege to participate.

"Now relax, Hooper." Hooper tried to relax. He sort of slumped his shoulders a bit. Professor Smith walked quietly over to Hooper and handed him the bundle of papers. "Now, just look up at the shelf and think about what I am going to say." Hooper looked up. And then Professor Smith started to speak so fast that he sounded like a record that had been put on the wrong speed. "A sweater, worn in the usual way, has a label on the inside of the collar. Assuming that the sleeve which accommodates the left arm when the sweater is worn normally is referred to as the left sleeve, where will the label be if the sweater is turned inside out, and the right arm is put into the left sleeve and the left arm is put into the right sleeve? Will the label be on the front outside. . . ?"

"Back outside," said Hooper, but he was mightily upset and confused. Moreover, he hadn't moved an inch higher.

"Excellent!" cried Professor Smith.

"How'd you know that so *fast?*" breathed October in awe. Blue and Athena said, "Gee!"

"I knew the answer," Hooper said. "You gave me that one before," he said to Professor Smith. "I worked it out at home with my own sweater." Professor Smith seemed very excited. "Now, would you like to try another?"

"Well, maybe, just one," said Hooper.

"Just one," Professor Smith said. "Let me see, now. All right. Let's say that one brick balances evenly in a scale with a three-quarter-pound weight and three-quarters of another brick. How much does the whole brick weigh?"

Hooper groaned. There were all those numbers to solve again. They were hard to remember, so he started to make a picture in his mind of a scale, but that reminded him of the carnival that had come to East Westham a few years ago. There was one act where a man had a scale and you could show the man any article—anything at all—and he would guess the weight. And if he was more than a few ounces off, you got a prize. You paid the man fifteen cents to play. Hooper had shown him a handful of marbles that he had in his pocket. The man guessed wrong. One of the marbles was made of heavy metal. Hooper had won a plastic water pistol, which, unfortunately, broke before the carnival was over.

And *now* suddenly Hooper's head hit the ceiling.

"Hurray!" cried Blue, while October and Athena clapped.

"What's the answer, Hooper?" asked Professor Smith.

"Haven't got it yet," admitted Hooper.

"Haven't got it yet!" exclaimed the Professor. "Fascinating! Puzzling, but fascinating!" and he sat down at his desk and started to make notes while Hooper laid the package of manuscripts on the shelf and looked down.

"Hey, great, Hooper!" said Blue. "But I promised my mother I'd be home by five. I can't wait for you. What are you going to do?"

"I guess I'll just hang around a while," said Hooper.

"See you, then," said Blue.

"I'll go tell your mother that you'll be a little late," said October practically.

Hooper lounged around the upper regions of Professor Smith's now well-ordered but nevertheless entirely chock-full room, peeking into the baskets he had noticed

"Hurray!" cried Blue.

on his first visit. In three or four, some odd plants grew healthily amid the warm damp pipes of the ceiling, winding themselves around the pipes in a very decorative fashion. One basket contained shells, some so enormous that Hooper could not imagine the sort of creature that had ever lived inside them. One basket was entirely full of dried seed pods. He skimmed over to the red raffia basket with the chain and lock. He touched it tentatively with one finger. It swayed lightly and Hooper thought he heard a rustling sound inside. *Could* it be a snake? "What's in here?" Hooper called down to Professor Smith. There was no answer.

It was nearly dusk when Hooper reached his normal skimming altitude. It may have been the sound of him adjusting his skates that alerted the Professor, or perhaps he was just finished. In any case, he spun around in his chair and said, "Oh dear! I entirely forgot about you, although there was nothing else on my mind. Forgive me. I shall accompany you right to your apartment-house door. Come along!"

"May I ask you a question?" asked Hooper as they approached his apartment house.

"Anything," said Professor Smith. "Answer, of course, is a different matter."

"Could I ask you what is in the red straw basket that is hanging from the pipe in the middle of your room? It's not important," he hurried to say. "It just sort of interests me, especially because of the chain."

A look of rapture came over Professor Smith. "In that basket," he said, "is a rare thing. It is a recipe for Swedish pancakes, which I adore, especially when heaped with loganberries and sprinkled with sugar."

"But then why do you keep the recipe on the ceiling?" asked Hooper. "It must be very hard to get."

"That's it!" said Professor Smith. "That's the whole idea. The pancakes do not agree with me—not in the numbers I tend to eat them. So I keep the recipe in a place where it is an infernal nuisance to reach. Then if the craving is *that* great, it takes a great deal of trouble and exercise to get it and then to put it back. I do wish you hadn't mentioned it, my boy. I had nearly forgotten about it for the week."

"I'm sorry," said Hooper.

"Can't be helped," said Professor Smith. "And here is where I leave you. See you soon again. *I think we may be on to something.*"

10

Within a few days, Mr. Toote set up a series of appointments for Hooper, for the purpose of investigating the most interesting of the offers.

"Now, not too much at once," cautioned Mrs. Toote. "The whole thing is just too unnatural." So Mr. Toote selected the two most promising. The first one was with Barton Brothers Circus.

"Oh, Hugh, a circus!" cried Mrs. Toote. "I just won't have it."

"Come on, Mum," said Hooper. "It's just to look and see. We won't do anything you don't want. We told you so."

"We told you that, first thing," said Mr. Toote, patting her shoulder. "You say no, and it's no go. Right, Hooper?"

"Right!" said Hooper. "But the *circus!* Oh boy!"

So Hooper and his father took the subway and the

tube under the Hudson River to Hoboken, where the circus was having a one-week stand on the outskirts of the city. They both felt marvelous as they approached the big top and whiffed the intoxicating odor of peanuts, popcorn, and assorted animals.

They went directly to the circus manager's office, which was in a gorgeous red trailer truck. The manager greeted them like visiting royalty.

"Aha!" he cried. "So this is the young man!" And he looked Hooper up and down and around, and his eyes lit up like spotlights. "Let's go into the tent and take a look at his act. Follow me."

"Act?" whispered Hooper to Mr. Toote. "What act?" Mr. Toote shrugged.

"He must think it's a stage trick," said Mr. Toote. "Well, just be your usual self, Hooper, that's all."

They followed the manager into the tent, which was still being prepared for the circus opening. They had to step over all kinds of striped props and buckets of paint and coils of rope, and wend their way around men sprinkling sawdust. Hooper stopped to watch a man wrestling with a lion, and to listen to the band rehearsing in a corner. His eye was caught, too, by a sight way up at the top of the tent—a lovely girl doing cartwheels on a tight wire.

"She's our star," the manager said. "Andromeda." He pointed to the sign near the entrance. It read:

BARTON BROS. STAR, ANDOMEDA

"That's not a star," said Hooper. "That's a constellation. Andromeda is the name of a constellation."

"That so?" said the manager, interested. "Well . . . " And though he seemed a bit doubtful, he went over to one of the handy buckets of red paint and changed the sign to read:

CONSTELLATION,
BARTON BROS. S̶T̶A̶R̶, ANDROMEDA

He stepped back to look at it, shrugged, and then said, "Okay, let's see your stuff," and he took a seat in the great empty grandstand. Mr. Toote sat beside him.

Hooper selected the nearest ring and just killed a little time by skimming around in small circles, trying to think what to do.

"It starts out slow," said the manager. "Needs more showmanship. But we can work that out, if we have to."

Hooper started to skim a few elaborate figure eights. He remembered that the last time he had skimmed up was when he had been working on the riddle that Professor Smith had given him the other day. Maybe he could try it again now. So, while continuing his figure eights and alternating them with small circles, Hooper started to work the puzzle. Now, these bricks . . . Once again he formed the scale in his mind. Now if he remembered, and he was pretty sure he did this time, the riddle said that one brick balanced evenly on the scale with a three-quarter-pound weight—Hooper put a three-quarter-pound weight on the scale in his mind—and then three-quarters of another brick. *How much did the whole brick weigh? Well, let's see . . . A quarter of a brick must weigh . . . uh . . . three-quarters of a pound. So then the whole brick must weigh four times that. Right? Right. And that was . . . um . . . hard. Three pounds!* He'd solved it!

He'd solved it, but he was still skimming figure eights at his normal skimming height.

"It's fair," said the manager. What does he do for a finale?"

Hooper skimmed in larger circles. He didn't know about the manager, but he was getting bored with this, himself. And then he looked up and saw Andromeda, the constellation, smiling down on him. She turned a dainty cartwheel on the tight wire and then took three or four beautifully balanced steps that brought her to the high platform where she stepped off the wire.

How delightful it looked up there! How *he* would love to be a real constellation—

BARTON BROS. CONSTELLATION, HOOPER TOOTE!

His mind could see it clearly. But Hooper Toote was, somehow, not an especially good name for a constellation. Perhaps Cepheus or Perseus? How about that? Perseus! Pretty good. Auriga? No, that wouldn't do. But wait! Now, he had it—Camelopardus!

BARTON BROS. NEWEST CONSTELLATION, CAMELOPARDUS

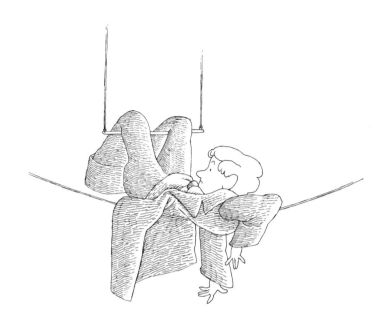

"You could get killed that way."

And suddenly Hooper realized that he was tangled in a maze of trapeze ropes and tight wires. Nearby, Andromeda had stopped turning cartwheels and was just staring.

"Hey kid!" she said, sounding not exactly as Hooper imagined a star would sound, and less like a constellation. "Neat trick! But you could get killed that way."

"Thanks," said Hooper, untangling himself from a rope.

"Here, want to use the wire?"

"Okay," said Hooper, shakily, not knowing what he would do with it. So the girl walked on the wire over to the platform. Hooper skimmed about until his feet were parallel to the wire. Then, holding his right foot straight ahead of the left, in the position he had seen the girl using, he started skimming over the wire as if it were greased.

"For heaven's sake!" cried Andromeda. "I can do something like that *downhill*, but straight across on a level . . . !"

"Sold!" shouted the manager, nearly beside himself with excitement. But then, recovering his business sense, he said to Mr. Toote, "Pending an agreement as to price, of course. Okay, kid, come down now. I have an appointment, so I'll go through your whole act another time."

Andromeda said, "Listen, I'll show you how to do the cartwheels if you show me that trick!"

Hooper smiled shyly, and gave a sort of ducking motion with his head that he thought straddled the issue nicely. It was neither yes nor no.

"So let me have the wire, now," said Andromeda, and Hooper obligingly skimmed off into the air, leaving the wire free. Andromeda nearly lost her footing on the platform when she saw him do it.

"What in the name of Barnum and Bailey are you doing!" she shrieked, waiting for him to plummet through the air to the tanbark beneath. But up he stayed, of course. And there was a problem.

"I can't get down," Hooper confided to Andromeda.

"Whatd'ya mean you can't get down? You ever hear of gravity?" As Hooper just seemed to stay suspended in space, Andromeda gave up trying to work out the mystery. She was used to astounding acts, even though this *was* pretty far out.

"Well, look, you just slide down on the rope," she called as she started turning her cartwheels again.

So Hooper skimmed over to the rope that performers used to slide down to the ground from the high trapezes. But he didn't *slide*. By an enormous effort of strength he pulled himself down, hand over hand, until he was nearly to the ground. Mr. Toote rushed over and grabbed him, slipped the extra-heavy weights into his pockets, and held on to him for the next hour.

"Come over to the office and we'll talk business," said the manager. "But we're going to have to do something about that floating routine. Even if it's a trick, it looks too easy. Not enough suspense. Customers like to be scared, you know."

"It's not a trick," said Hooper. The manager chucked him under the chin and laughed.

But Mr. Toote was in command. "Write us your offer, please," he said. "We'll have other offers to consider in the meantime."

The manager looked shocked. "I'm going to give you top money," he said. "Top money. Don't worry about that."

"That's what we want, all right," said Hooper, a bit light-headed from his debut at the circus and his encounter with a genuine constellation. Oddly, he seemed to lose some of his buoyancy each time the manager said "top money." Or perhaps he only seemed to.

"Now, you let me handle this, Hooper," said Mr. Toote. "Just write us your best offer," he said to the manager, "and we'll call you. Don't call us," he added. The manager sputtered a bit as they left. Hooper called good-bye to Andromeda, who gave him a starry wave.

11

It was well into August when Mr. Toote arranged for the meeting with NASA, the National Aeronautics and Space Administration in Washington, D.C.

"Does that mean I'll be an astronaut?" asked Hooper.

"Not necessarily," said Mr. Toote.

"Now, Hugh," cautioned Mrs. Toote. "Remember your promise. I will not have Hooper being sent for trips to the moon or Mars." But Mrs. Toote was maturing. "Not until we know more about it, at least," she said.

"Atta girl!" said Mr. Toote, and they were off for Washington, D.C., where some officials of NASA had arranged a meeting. Hooper had one morning's look at Washington while waiting for the appointment, and he thought that if only his father could have skimmed, they might have seen a lot more. However, he did not say so, because he did not wish to hurt his father's feelings. Mr. Toote, Hooper fully appreciated, was putting himself to a great deal of trouble, even neglecting his own work in order to look into and carefully consider these offers.

The NASA people were all dressed up in army, navy, and air force uniforms. There were a few civilians, too, and a man in a white coat who, Hooper learned, was some sort of scientist. Hooper didn't quite know what use the white coat was, but by the same token the other uniforms did not seem particularly useful either.

They all sat down around a big polished conference table in a big, well-guarded room, high up in a big stone government building, with large windows open to a beautiful view of the Washington Monument. Hooper slipped into a seat between his father and a man named General Olifant.

"The reason for our interest," began General Olifant, "is obvious."

Mr. Toote nodded.

"Whatever it is that causes your son to behave as he does should be applicable to others."

"In other words—" said the scientist, and then he looked warily at the general. "If I may, General?"

"Right ahead," said General Olifant.

"In other words, then, the aberration should be able to be synthesized, somehow, in the laboratory."

Mr. Toote nodded, as did Hooper, but he had only a vague idea of what had been said. It sounded good, though.

"This is strictly confidential, of course," said General Olifant.

"In other words—" said the scientist.

"Of course," said Mr. Toote.

"Our thought was that, in traversing the surface of the moon now—and planets, who knows when—we would not have to worry about the kind of surface, if our astronauts could . . . um . . . hover."

"Skim," corrected Hooper.

"Skim," said General Olifant.

Although the talk sounded important, it seemed to be going across Hooper and around him, and he felt strangely uncomfortable in the big room, in the big building, with all these big people. The room was hot and tense; the talk had a lot of words in it that Hooper did not understand, although "space" and "moon" kept sifting through. The voices at the conference table faded into the background, but he heard, vaguely, ". . . he will demonstrate his technique, and . . ."

And that set Hooper to worrying. It had been bothering him just how he was going to demonstrate anything. The riddle hadn't worked at the circus. But then somehow he *had* skimmed up to the high wire with Andromeda. Wow! What a day that had been at the circus! He could be the youngest constellation ever, if he wanted to be, probably. Or if he joined NASA, he could be the youngest astronaut ever, maybe . . . leading men across the moon . . . a sort of scout. But then, if he joined the circus, maybe he could wear an astronaut suit (with spangles on it, of course) and have a moon for a prop instead of a trapeze. What an idea! What an act! CAMELOPARDUS, THE FIRST ASTRONAUT UNDER THE BIG TOP.

The NASA people were all standing, looking up with the looks people usually had on their faces when they saw Hooper suspended comfortably in the air above them.

"Oh, zounds!" said General Olifant. "Never mind anything else. Come on down," and he turned to the rest of the members of the NASA conference and resumed his part in the talk. "Zounds!" he said again.

"Right," said the man in the white coat. "I'd like that young man to skim at my laboratory at nine tomorrow morning for some exhaustive testing."

"Oh, now, just a minute," said Mr. Toote. "We have made no arrangements and no commitments whatever."

General Olifant waved his arm to ward off protests.

"Just a matter of simple red tape," he said. "We'll get him on the army payroll, or we'll get a civil service rating for him, or some such thing, though heaven only knows how to write up the job description."

And while they were splitting Hooper up among themselves, Hooper skimmed slowly over to the window for a look at the magnificent vista of Washington, D.C., which was certainly an even handsomer city when viewed from a height. He could see for miles—miles out and miles up into the clear day. He poked his head out for a really good look to the left for a clear view of the Capitol with its beautiful dome. And then, before anyone realized it, least of all Hooper (who was still admiring the Capitol), he had drifted out the open window, over Lafayette Park, across Pennsylvania Avenue, down across the White House rose garden, where something gala was going on, and then he started in the general direction of the Washington Monument.

As soon as the situation was apprehended and assimilated by the group in the top-secret conference, the air force general took command. He reached for a red, white, and blue telephone and snapped into it, controlling hysteria very well, "May Day! May Day! Airborne alert! Send helicopter pursuit to intercept flying object . . . repeat . . . *friendly* flying object. Over! Roger! Approaching Washington Monument. Proceed as directed. That is all. Come on, men. This may blow the whole thing sky-high!"

"Cat's out of the bag, eh?" asked Mr. Toote, but he

*He started in the direction
of the Washington Monument.*

was mostly worried about Hooper, who didn't know his
way around Washington, D.C.

General Olifant was muttering something about ". . .
aid and comfort to the enemy . . ." as the whole party
loaded themselves into several large, black limousines,
and with a police escort, sirens blaring, they started to
race Hooper to the Washington Monument. They took
the elevator to the top with the nearly hopeless hope of
catching him as he skimmed by.

But Hooper had changed course. He started due south, then switched a bit west toward a large five-sided building which he recognized as the fabled Pentagon.

Meanwhile pursuit helicopters appeared in the air and several people raised their heads to see what was going on. Things looked pretty normal for Washington, so they went back to whatever they were doing. The people in the rose garden complained of the excess noise, and the First Lady sent word to have the helicopters move off.

As for Hooper, he had never in his life skimmed so high. When he became fully aware of his situation, his exhilaration and delight were marred by a slight apprehension. Since he had never been this far off the ground, he had no idea how long it might be before he would drift down. Tomorrow, at least, he thought. And he did not look forward to spending the night in the air over Washington, D.C. There were a good many things to bump into, for one thing, and his father might be worrying about him, for another. Also, ahead of him lay a body of water—the Potomac River!

But he was diverted from his worries by the marvelous panorama. From this particular height and point of view, the world below looked spectacularly beautiful—unusually interesting, like a strange place seen, perhaps, in a motion picture or in a dream. There was certainly a lot more to a city than you could tell from the street. And what could possibly be going on in all those buildings? So this is what the newspapers and radio and TV always meant when they announced "News from Washington!" As he circled the Pentagon several times he wondered if there might be an office in that enormous building that was in charge of history. If so, perhaps when he got down he could pay a call and ask *them* all these questions about the Hundred Years' War that were bothering him, and . . .

And this is when Hooper became aware of all the helicopters swirling in very close. He didn't want to tangle with any helicopters. Skimming this high had its problems. And then he saw one of the helicopters deliberately rise to a spot above him and just hover there. And then a sort of basket started to descend from the 'copter, just like the recovery teamwork Hooper had seen on TV. The pilot leaned out and motioned to Hooper. Hooper got the idea, and right now, it seemed like a pretty good one. He skimmed over to the basket and sat in it. They reeled him in just like an astronaut. It was one of the dandiest experiences he had ever had.

"What you doin', boy?" the helicopter pilot asked him.

"Just looking around," said Hooper.

"Where you from?" asked the pilot.

"New York," said Hooper.

"Yeah!" said the pilot, who knew when to stop asking questions. But he went on, under his breath, "Yeah, yeah, yeah!"

Hooper enjoyed the way the helicopter landed, hovering, hovering, hovering, and lowering until it was right on the mark. Hooper thought he might be able to learn something from that. But after that, things began to happen fast. The helicopter door was flung open and he was met by a large crowd of military people in odd gauze face masks.

The limousine, despite its escort, was several minutes later in its arrival than the helicopter and not in time to prevent the processing of Hooper by his unusual reception committee. Hooper, regrettably, had been wrapped in plastic, capped with a masked helmet, and put into an isolation tank.

"Sorry, sir," said an air force aide worriedly when he was informed by the furious air force general that Hooper was *not* contaminated with outer planetary dust. "Our message said 'unfriendly flying object.' "

"I distinctly said 'friendly,' " said the general. "Don't you know the difference between friendly and unfriendly?"

"I think so, sir," said the aide.

But the army's General Olifant was wasting no time disciplining subordinates. He called his own aide and dictated a memorandum on the spot.

"For immediate release to all newspapers, radio stations, and television networks. Quote: Contrary to rumors, it was a combination of sun spots, smog, and hysteria that created the effect of some unidentified flying object over Washington, D.C. today, a reliable source at the Pentagon reported. End quote. There! That should do it."

"Well, let's just get some appointments set up now,"

the scientist said when he saw that the crisis was under control. But Mr. Toote was still checking Hooper over for possible damage, and was just getting over his own considerable feelings of worry.

"Just write us the details, please," he said. "We'll think it over."

"Think it over!" cried General Olifant. "This is a clear national duty."

"We'll take that fact into consideration," said Mr. Toote. "But if Hooper does it, it will be because he wants to. And besides, we have to ask his mother."

"Besides, the circus wants me," said Hooper.

"Circus!" cried General Olifant, "when we are offering you the moon!" And he said it at the same time that the admiral was rolling up his eyes and whispering hoarsely, "Ask his mother!"

"Why, yes, the circus," replied Mr. Toote. "I'll bet even you would have liked to join a circus when you were young."

"Well, yes, I did want to," agreed the general. "But, my dear sir, you have to realize that, at that time, there wasn't any moon!"

12

After the climactic day in and over Washington, Hooper found it hard getting back into the swing of things. There was something strange about looking up or straight at people instead of down . . . up at buildings instead of down on them . . . that affected Hooper. He skated along the street by himself just looking at things that he hadn't noticed much before—small things, big things. An old woman scolding her cat. A child playing a wonderful game all by herself, bouncing a ball against both sides of a door frame. Hooper wanted to ask her to show him how, but he didn't. He stood for a long while watching some men dig a hole in the street with a jackhammer. It made a lot of noise, but then he got a really good look down into the hole and saw all the stuff that was under the pavement—pipes, and big cylinders of cement, and also just a lot of space with junk. A man climbed down and started to fix a pipe. It looked like a hot, hard job.

Hooper wandered down among the shops and stared for a time at a man who was sitting quite still in a jeweler's window. He had his face so close to a watch he was fixing that his nose was nearly resting on the work table. The man had more patience than Hooper. Hooper left.

He walked way over to the river and watched men in blue shirts, which turned black as they worked, loading a barge. He watched the barge start down the river, pushed by a small strong tugboat. Where was it going? But Hooper didn't ask anyone.

He went to the museum and skimmed about for a couple of hours through one big room of wonders after another. He wandered through an Egyptian tomb and saw writings on the walls that looked like the butcher's bill he had seen at Professor Smith's. He saw a whole bowl of a beautiful orangey color, like one of the fragments Professor Smith had. " . . . almost five thousand years ago," the Professor had said. Hooper tried to imagine a straight line going from five thousand years ago until now. On one end of the line was the bowl and on the other end was Hooper Toote. How long would the line be?

Hooper went out into the late afternoon sunshine and took a leaflet from a man in a long robe with a sparkly band around his forehead. The leaflet read, "The Time Has Come." Hooper put the leaflet in his pocket.

Hooper was very quiet for a couple of days. He did not go to the park to skate or to look for his friends. He was so quiet that Mrs. Toote suggested that it might be a good idea to ask Professor Smith to tea. "It's high time we met him, Hooper," she said. "How about going over and asking him if he would like to join us for a late afternoon snack? I'll just cut a few sandwiches and put some cookies in the oven."

"Okay," said Hooper, perking up a little. He had wanted to talk with Professor Smith, but he wasn't just sure what he wanted to say. So much had been going through his mind without any really complete thoughts. Everything seemed sort of mixed up again.

Professor Smith, it turned out, was delighted with the invitation. "Just have to find my other black shoe and I'll be right with you," he said. "Been wearing one black and one brown one for days." Hooper took off his skates and helped look behind the stacks of papers and under chairs. "How are things, my boy? Good trip?"

"Yes," said Hooper absently, lying on his stomach—or at least *skimming* on his stomach—to look under the bed. "It was a good trip. I'll tell you about it. But first, could you tell me where the barges go, down there at the dock?"

"Oh, everywhere, I should think," said Professor Smith. "Out to sea, down the coast, into the blue. Depends what's on 'em." He climbed on a chair to look behind the refrigerator. "All sorts of things fall off the top of the refrigerator," he explained. Hooper knew that, but he had never known a shoe to do it.

"What does it mean . . ." Hooper fished in his pocket

for the leaflet that the man in the long robe had given him. "What does it mean, 'The Time Has Come'?" Professor Smith reached down and took the leaflet.

"Ah, yes. Well, that means the person who gave it to you has an idea in his head that he wants to tell you about."

"But what is his idea?" asked Hooper.

"Obviously he thinks that the time has come. For what? For what, he does not say. Perhaps he does not know, or perhaps the time has come for something different for everyone." And then the Professor found the shoe. It had been propping up the bent stalk of a large philodendron plant. They put a pile of books beside the philodendron instead, and Professor Smith was now able to start putting on a pair of matching shoes.

"Maybe it doesn't mean anything," said Hooper.

"What? The time has come?" The Professor thought about it while he started working on the laces of his left shoe. "Oh, I don't think anything is entirely without meaning. We may just not know the meaning."

"But what if I want to know?" urged Hooper.

"Then," said Professor Smith, "you will just have to set about finding out. Could be a career in itself. Have you given much thought to the sort of thing you might really like to do . . . someday . . . in the future?"

"Well, I'm thinking of the circus, of course," said Hooper.

"Ah, yes, of course," the Professor said, almost as if he had forgotten it.

"And now NASA," Hooper said. "I'm thinking about being an astronaut. But there's a lot going on around here. I've been looking . . ."

"NASA!" cried the Professor. "Now, don't lose another minute. I want to hear about that visit."

Then Hooper spilled out the words every which way, jumping from one thing to another. He ended with an account of the general who had dictated the news release to his aide, when there had been all that excitement after the helicopter landing.

Professor Smith gave up tying his shoe for a moment. "So *you* were the unidentified flying object that the radio announced was *not* seen over Washington that day! This is mighty interesting. Mighty! A rare experience, that was—actually hearing a fable being written to explain fact!" The Professor was excited. "Now you see, *that* was the sort of thing I was telling you about Richard the Third and the little princes in the tower. *Muddled!* Remember? See, there was a case where the written facts contradicted each other and, perhaps, the truth. Indeed, the truth may never be known."

"But we know the truth about this—about me," said Hooper.

"We do," said Professor Smith worriedly, "but there are those hundreds of newspapers and all that radio and television news that proclaimed that mass hysteria or sun spots produced the effect of a flying object over Washington, D.C. By gum, if I really thought it would make some difference (and if anyone would bail me out of the loony bin) I'd go and tell them myself that that was no sun spot." Professor Smith waved his right shoe in the air. "That was Hooper Toote, skimmer extraordinary, having a day on the town."

"It was exciting," Hooper said.

Professor Smith was still considering the matter. Finally he said, "After serious thought, I think, in this case, the matter should have no far-reaching historical consequences. But it still makes my blood boil. I don't know . . . I just might . . . " He was putting on his shoe again.

"Historical consequences!" Hooper said. "You mean like yesterday was *history*?"

"Exactly that," Professor Smith answered. "Yesterday *was*, today *is* history," and he stared off at the feet going by his front windows and mumbled a bit, mostly to himself. "And we had better make it a pretty good story, I'd say."

"But how?" Hooper asked, because mumble or not, Hooper was paying close attention. The idea of being a real piece of history was intriguing.

"Oh heavens!" Professor Smith was pensive. "If I really knew that, I wouldn't be inventing buttonhooks. In my mind, it seems all we need to do is work at it, you know—honest, straight, hard. Call a razor blade a razor blade, an identified flying object an identified flying object." He gestured helplessly.

"But that's not hard," said Hooper.

"You wouldn't think so, would you?" Professor Smith was dreaming again, and Hooper wondered if the right shoe was ever going to get all the way on. "I didn't think so myself, once. No, you wouldn't really think it would be hard . . . to make history just the way we all want it . . . with all the things we know, and know how to do. You would think we could make it nearly perfect . . . for everyone."

"I'd like to do that," said Hooper. "Make it perfect for everyone." And then, with a sudden decision that was nearly as startling in its effect as his first attack, "*That's* what I'd really like to do. That's what I want to do when I grow up. But now—maybe I could . . . Do you think . . . ?"

And then Professor Smith noted a change in Hooper's expression, and he followed his gaze down . . . down . . . down to the cuffs of the pants that Mrs. Toote had so carefully tailored to cover the space between Hooper and the floor around Hooper's feet. And Hooper's feet . . . Hooper's feet were firmly planted on the floor of Professor Smith's room.

"Ah, then!" the Professor finally said, letting out a long-held breath. Hooper found himself with absolutely nothing to say. He just sampled the floor with his shoes, wiggling his toes, pressing with his heels. There was no question about it. *Hooper was standing.*

Professor Smith spoke quietly. "I believe," he said, "that if you try, right now, you could walk."

Hooper stood still, just wiggling his toes. For the first time in his life he was really nervous. It seemed to him that in the last month there had been more "first things" in his life than in all the rest of his life. New experiences and feelings had been piling up one on top of the other so fast—New York, H. G. Wells, skating, Blue and his other new friends, Professor Smith and all the interesting and exciting things he had learned from him, the circus, NASA, the helicopter trip, his recent quiet tours of the city . . . and now *this*! Just at the moment, anything else was too much. "Not just this minute," he said. "Not just now, if you please."

"Whenever you're ready," Professor Smith said. "Whenever you're ready." He finished putting on his shoe, and then he brought Hooper his skates.

The Professor accompanied Hooper as he skated slowly home. Hooper did not feel at all like himself. He said nothing at all and the Professor did not interrupt the quiet. It was interrupted, though, when they arrived at the Tootes' apartment. Mr. Toote came to greet them. Mrs. Toote followed close behind.

"Welcome to you, Professor Smith," said Mr. Toote, extending his hand and then giving Hooper a fatherly pat on the shoulder. "Hi, Hooper," he said.

"How good of you to come on such short notice," said Mrs. Toote. "We've been looking forward to meeting you."

Professor Smith looked sideways at Hooper, who remained quiet. "What's that gorgeous smell?" the Professor asked then. "Oh, my, fresh cookies!" He had followed the aroma to the kitchen. "My dear Mrs. Toote, would it be too much of an imposition to ask to let me scrape the bowl?" He had caught sight of the nearly empty bowl of cookie batter. "It must be forty years or more since I have scraped a cookie bowl. Fifty, perhaps. Fifty years without scraping one cookie bowl."

Mrs. Toote was sympathetic and offered him a spoon, but he said he preferred his fingers. He swept them

Mrs. Toote noticed it immediately.

126

around the bowl, whipping up the scraps of soft dough, with a look on his face as if someone had just told him a beautiful secret.

"I suppose Hooper has told you all about Washington," said Mr. Toote. "That was quite a day, wasn't it, Hooper?"

Hooper nodded.

"As a matter of fact," Professor Smith now said deliberately, "today seems to be quite a day, eh, Hooper?"

"What is it, son?" asked Mr. Toote with interest. "What happened?"

Hooper said nothing, but bent down and unbuckled his skates. Then he stood up. The cuffs of his trousers fell around his ankles as if he were wearing pants that belonged to a tall uncle who had kindly handed them down to him.

Mrs. Toote noticed it immediately. "Dear me!" she said. "I hadn't noticed that those trousers were so baggy."

Mr. Toote looked down too. Then Mrs. Toote suddenly drew in her breath and said, "Oh, Hooper!"

There was silence.

Then Mr. Toote slowly got down on his knees and lifted Hooper's trousers cuffs.

13

"The time has come . . ." said the Professor, picking up the last of the cookies without the least embarrassment. "Delicious," he said for the twentieth time, to the delight of Mrs. Toote. The Tootes were getting over the shock of that first sight of Hooper on his feet, and considerable thought and conversation had accompanied the afternoon tea. It covered Hooper's past and Hooper's present. It touched on fact, possibility, and probability. As for Hooper, he had simply lowered himself to the floor and remained there, cross-legged, thinking a lot and talking a little. But when Professor Smith said, "The time has come," he looked up.

"The time has come," Hooper said. "I wonder . . ."

"Indeed, you might well wonder," said Professor Smith.

"Oh, dear," said Mrs. Toote. "I seem to have lost

128

track of the conversation. I'm sorry, but I really am so distracted by this change in Hooper. It was so unexpected."

"Not entirely," said Professor Smith. "It could be guessed at. There were some hints. But I admit I really did not expect anything this immediate. The boy has a very quick mind, I think."

"But what has Hooper's quick mind got to do with it?" asked Mr. Toote.

"He's always had the same mind. I'm sure of that," said Mrs. Toote with her usual confidence in Hooper.

"True," said Professor Smith, "but my theory—and it's *only* a theory based on a lot of unscientific guesswork—my theory is that Hooper's mind has not really been fully used before. He was able but untried, shall we say. Whatever he did was fairly easy for him, or . . ."

"Oh, that's very true," Mrs. Toote agreed.

"Well, of course this all needs to be explored more fully," Professor Smith continued, "but first I must confess that, as a scientist, I am a bungler and very plodding and slow. I may be able to show the 'why' of all this long after it matters at all. But I do have some ideas."

"But what are your ideas?" asked Mr. Toote.

"Well, in the beginning, of course, I went through the obvious ideas—that this was purely kinetic. That is, that it had something to do with the way Hooper moved or stood or some position that he unconsciously took that made him skim up. But that was an idea I quickly discarded when I hit on the riddle theory."

"The riddle theory!" cried Mrs. Toote.

"He had me doing all kind of riddles," Hooper said with enthusiasm. "Really good ones. I'm going to try them on you, Pop."

"Okay," said Mr. Toote, "but not until we get back to normal. Just what was your riddle theory?" he asked Professor Smith.

"Well, it was based on the notion that the riddle, which you, yourself, gave him, had something to do with his skimming the day he went up the apartment building and started the stir."

"But I never solved that riddle," Hooper reminded the Professor.

"But you did get us into the apartment, Hooper," said Mrs. Toote.

"That's true," Hooper said, "but . . . "

"I wanted to explore that notion, so I tried out some other riddles on Hooper. There *seemed* to be something in it."

"And *was* there?" asked Mr. Toote. "Was it the riddle that made him skim up?"

"Only indirectly," Professor Smith answered. "At least that is what I think now. He didn't solve the riddle, but he did skim up. What was the relationship?"

"What?" asked Mrs. Toote promptly.

"I did solve the puzzle about the bricks, though," interrupted Hooper.

"You did!" Professor Smith was very interested. "When was that?"

"At the circus. The answer is three pounds. I tried to work it out then, because I remembered you said you thought we might 'be on to something.' "

"And *did* it make you skim up?" urged Professor Smith. "Did it?"

"No."

"Just as I thought." Professor Smith looked very pleased. "And now I'll tell you why I think it did not. Because it was work . . . *hard* work. And you were *doing* it! You were working on it, not skimming away from it!"

Hooper thought about it. "But I was trying to work on the others, too. The one about the sweater, when you first gave it to me, and the one about the sultan that my father gave me."

"But were you?" asked Professor Smith. "I wonder, those other times that you were 'working' on the riddles, if you were really trying hard enough to solve them. Perhaps—now, this is just a perhaps—but perhaps you even stopped trying to solve them and . . ."

"Maybe," Hooper admitted. "I did get kind of muddled, especially if there were numbers, you know."

"Yet, at the circus," Professor Smith pressed on, "after you did the puzzle and *didn't* skim up . . . then later, you *did* skim way up, didn't you! Why? What did you do?"

"Nothing," said Hooper. "I was just skimming around and around, trying to think of something interesting to do for the act, and then there was this really beautiful acrobat doing cartwheels on the high wire. And I was wishing . . ."

"Wishing!" said the Professor. "Hooper! What were you wishing?"

Hooper honestly tried to think back. "Well, mostly I was wishing I could be a constellation like her," he confessed. "I even thought of a name for myself—Camelopardus!"

"Camelopardus!" breathed Professor Smith.

"You like it!" Hooper exclaimed with pleasure.

"Yes, yes! But do you mean you dreamed it up, right *there* . . . then?"

"Yes. At first I thought of some others . . ."

Professor Smith smiled. "Hooper, do you think it would be fair to say that you were, at the time, wool-gathering . . . *daydreaming?*"

"Maybe," Hooper admitted. "But you should have seen it! You would have liked to do it yourself. It's not easy, you know. First, I got all tangled up in the wires. Then I had to figure how to . . ."

Professor Smith was doing a bit of wool-gathering himself. "I know I would have liked it, Hooper," he said. "It's just the sort of thing I would have liked at your age. Yet, instead, my own escapes took me out to the garage workshop where I daydreamed glorious inventions."

"Escapes!" exclaimed Mrs. Toote.

"If you understand my meaning of the word," said Professor Smith, returning from his own childhood to the present. "I am led to believe now that Hooper has been using daydreams and diversions to escape—in *his* case, to skim up—from whatever happened to be the problem at hand at the moment, whether the problem was a riddle or a matter he preferred not to cope with . . . like that fight on the playground back in East Westham."

"Or the spelling bee," recalled Mrs. Toote. "But *friable*! Really!"

"Well, let's see," the Professor said. "For example, what were you doing the other day, Hooper, when you hit your head on the ceiling at NASA?"

"Nothing," said Hooper. "Just the usual thing."

"The same kind of 'nothing' that skimmed you up to the top of the circus tent?" asked Professor Smith.

Hooper thought back. "Like that, maybe," he said. "You see, I wasn't sure how to . . . well . . . 'demonstrate my skills' is what they said. And then . . . now I remember . . . I got this great idea for doing a moon act for the circus. Wouldn't that be cool!"

"Cool," said Professor Smith. "And then?"

"Then I hit the ceiling, and after that . . ."

"Oh heavens!" said Mr. Toote, recollecting the whole thing, himself. "We know what happened after that, and I'm not anxious to go through it again. I tell you I thought Hooper was on his way down the Potomac River."

"It's getting dangerous now, really!" Mrs. Toote said anxiously.

"Yes, it was," Professor Smith agreed.

"Was!" said Mr. Toote. "You mean . . . you mean

133

you don't think Hooper is going to skim . . . anymore?"
Hooper's eyes were wonder-round.

"Can't answer that with any degree of authority," said
Professor Smith. "No precedents for this, you know. But
it does seem less predictable and controllable, doesn't it?
That flight over Washington, D.C. gives you just an
idea. And now this new development . . ." He glanced at
Hooper still sitting cross-legged, flat on the floor. "Just
for the moment, let us think of Hooper's new situation.
And let us talk about . . . um . . . horizons."

"Horizons!" cried Mrs. Toote, to whom the horizon
had always been an imaginary line where earth and sky
met.

"Yes, there are all kinds of horizons and we all have
some—horizons of interest, horizons of hopes, aims, am-
bitions. Oh, dear!" The Professor found himself standing with his hands folded across his chest. "I'm lecturing.
I forget whether I'm in a class or not when I get carried
away with an idea. You see . . ." he sat down again.
"Hooper's horizons are widening now. New things are
opening up to him all over the place—a new city, a new
school soon, new friends, new ideas, knowledge of the
past . . ."

"History," Hooper said solemnly.

"Knowledge of the present," the Professor continued.

"Did you know that today is history?" Hooper asked
his parents. "I'm thinking of being a part of history."

Mrs. Toote blinked. "That might be very nice, Hooper."

Professor Smith smiled. "Well, it wouldn't surprise me," he said. "I think he will be finding a new way to use his daydreams . . . not so much up and out—which is a dimension he has always had to *his* horizons—but I think he is finding exciting new horizons right here on this plane that we are all . . . well, stuck on, so to speak."

Mr. Toote, who had never considered himself particularly stuck, frowned and did a few jogs in place to show himself that he was, in fact, not in the least stuck.

"What I am saying," the Professor hurried on, "is that I think Hooper may find that what is happening here includes him . . . and his future. Simply put, Hooper is growing up. Could be as simple as that. Indeed, long scientific tests might prove only that—that where a child may wish, a man may act. It may be one of the consolations of growing up."

Hooper looked troubled. "But the moon," he said, "and NASA?"

"Well, they're there," Professor Smith said. He looked at Hooper still flat on the floor. "But at the moment, you are a bit earthbound, aren't you? And I have an idea that you may even decide that you prefer to be a person *of* the earth rather than above it. And as you grow, there is the possibility, indeed likelihood, that you will become, more definitely, a heavier-than-aircraft. Then your daydreams will not skim you away, but only do for you what daydreams do for all of us."

"For all of us?" asked Mrs. Toote.

"Help make things happen," said Professor Smith.

"There will be the Smith Levitational Shoe!"

"Make the impossible possible. Tide us over." But seeing Hooper's troubled frown, he said, "But who knows! You might always skim a little. Indeed, perhaps we all shall!" He looked delighted with the idea. "And if not, one day, of course, there will be the Smith Levitational Shoe!"

Hooper considered this with interest and then said,

"Maybe if I learned some real tricks like Andromeda, I could just make some guest appearances at the circus." He looked at his father. In his mind he saw a sign in front of the main tent—

TODAY ONLY, BARTON BROS.
GUEST CONSTELLATION, CAMELOPARDUS.

"Well, maybe we could have that written into a contract," said Mr. Toote. "I'll look into it."

"And sometimes," Mrs. Toote said cheerfully, "we might all go for a nice picnic and you might try skimming just for the fun of it, if you feel like it."

"Good idea!" said Mr. Toote. "Jones Beach would be the place."

"Oh, not Jones Beach, Hugh," cried Mrs. Toote. "All that water!"

"Oh, we'd have him on a line, you know," said Mr. Toote. "Reel him out and reel him in, like a kite. Don't want him joining up with any flock of sea gulls," and he laughed. Mrs. Toote didn't laugh.

The doorbell rang and Mrs. Toote went to answer it. Blue's voice could be heard, with October and Athena chiming in. "Is Hooper here? We haven't seen him for a lot of days."

"He's here," said Mrs. Toote, hesitating for just a moment. "But let me see if he's planning to come out just now." She left the door ajar. October stepped inside and smiled at Hooper. Hooper smiled back. She was a pretty nice girl.

There was silence in the room. Afternoon sunshine came through the long windows and fell upon Hooper, still sitting cross-legged on the floor. He stayed there for a moment, not moving. Then slowly . . . slowly . . . very slowly he stood up, just testing. His shoes were firmly upon the floor. He looked around at his mother, his father, and Professor Smith. He slid one foot experimentally ahead of the other and shifted his weight. He lifted the back foot and moved it ahead of the front foot. And then, balancing delicately, Hooper Toote, at the age of eleven going on twelve, took his first step.